BREAKING LORCA

BREAKING LORCA

GILES BLUNT

RANDOM HOUSE CANADA

www.randomhouse.ca

Random House Canada and colophon are trademarks

This book is a work of fiction. Names, characters, places, and incidents either are the product of the author's imagination or are used fictitiously. Any resemblance to actual persons, living or dead, events, or locales is entirely coincidental.

Library and Archives Canada Cataloguing in Publication

Blunt, Giles
    Breaking Lorca / Giles Blunt.

ISBN 978-0-307-35700-7

    I. Title.

PS8553.L867B75 2009   C813'.54   C2008-904130-5

Text design by Leah Springate

Printed and bound in the United States of America

10 9 8 7 6 5 4 3 2 1

PART ONE

I have shut my windows.
I do not want to hear the weeping.
But from behind the grey walls.
Nothing is heard but the weeping.

—FEDERICO GARCÍA LORCA

ONE

SOONER OR LATER the other soldiers in the squad were going to kill him. It was only a matter of time. Victor had never done anything to antagonize the brutes he worked with, but he was sure they hated him, or soon would.

He had wanted such a different life. He had wanted to be a teacher, but war had come and schools were closed. Many teachers were killed, many disappeared. Both of Victor's parents were dead; he had joined the army out of necessity. Now all he wanted was to stay alive.

He tried to concentrate on the paperback in his hand. Victor was reading *Of Mice and Men*—very slowly, and with an English–Spanish dictionary—but even reading at this turtle's pace, he was touched by the loyalty between the two men: big, dumb Lenny and shrewd, crabby George. John Steinbeck knew that people should exist in pairs. Victor would have given anything for a friend, someone to be loyal to, but there was no one like that in this place.

A friend might have helped stem the tide of fear that rose around him; he could feel it lapping at his chin. Soon the waters would close over his mouth and nose and he would drown altogether. The Captain hated him to be reading, he knew that, but there was simply no other way, lacking a friend, that he could distract himself from the fear that—maybe not for a month, maybe not for two—the other soldiers were going to kill him.

In America, now, things would be different. They had jobs in America, not war. You didn't have to carry a rifle to prove your manhood. He could go to a vast American city and lose himself among the crowds. No one would know what a coward he was. He would work at two jobs, three if necessary, and perhaps one day open a restaurant or a store. Maybe New York, maybe Washington, he hadn't decided yet. That was the nice thing about a fantasy, there were no decisions to make. He devoted himself to the study of English, knowing that one day he would speak it in America. Oh, all of the soldiers spoke a little English, but none of them could read it—he wasn't even sure if his uncle could read it.

Not that he could lose himself for long in fantasy, not at the little school. The air was sour with the smell of bodily fluids. The guardroom was a tiny space between the cells and the interrogation room. Pretty much the only thing the soldier on guard had to do was to bring the latrine bucket to the cells as needed, and to shoot anyone who tried to escape. There was no chance of that. Guard duty was easy, but the stench from the cells was not something you could forget for more than a few minutes at a time.

"Reading again." The Captain filled the entire doorway, casting a shadow over the book.

"Yes. Same story," Victor said, showing the cover. Anger emanated from his uncle like heat from a stove.

Captain Peña did not even glance at the book. "That's why you took guard duty, I suppose. Even though it's not your turn."

"The others enjoy their card games. I thought, why not let them?"

"You don't do it for them. You do it because you want to read."

"Well, yes," he said with what he hoped was a disarming smile. "Reading is definitely my vice."

"Don't imagine you're making friends by taking extra duty. You read in here because you don't want to be with them. You think they don't know that?"

"They like cards, I like books. Why is that a problem?"

"Don't be stupid. They know you are from a different class. By reading, you rub their noses in it."

"I don't think I'm better than them."

"Then you're even stupider than I thought. With your background and education? Of course you are better than them. But you're a corporal, not a general, and from now on you take your breaks like everybody else. You spend your free time with your brothers-in-arms."

"It's just going to cause trouble, sir. They don't want me around."

"They never will, if you don't make the effort."

A prisoner called out, "Please. I need the bucket. I can't wait any longer."

Victor started to get up.

"Sit down. I'm talking to you."

Victor sat down.

"I'm beginning to wonder why I saved your ass. I should have let Casarossa put you in front of that firing squad."

"Please don't think I'm ungrateful, sir. I'm very grateful." That was true. He was still amazed that his uncle, whom he had never known all that well, had saved him.

"I didn't do it for you. What would your father do if he knew he had a coward for a son?"

"He would have shot me himself," Victor said. "He would have had no mercy."

"Exactly. You didn't deserve any. That fake wound on your head."

"The wound was not fake, sir. I ran into a guy wire."

"Very convenient to fall into a ditch just when the fire-fight is about to begin. Quite a coincidence."

"I can't say. I don't know what happened."

"Oh, of course not. You were unconscious through the whole thing."

The prisoner called out again, "Please. The bucket. I can't hold out any longer."

Victor started to stand.

His uncle screamed so that the veins stood out on his neck. "You get up when I tell you to get up and not before! You think our dainty little prisoners need a bucket every time they whine for one? Forget the prisoners. The prisoners are dogs."

"Yes, sir."

"Dogs." The Captain took out a handkerchief and mopped his brow. He spoke more softly, as if he had suddenly remembered they were blood relatives. "I blame myself for letting things slide. Two weeks go by and you don't make the slightest effort to fit in. Well, things are going to change, understand?"

"Yes, sir."

"Number one: no more reading. Is that clear?"

"Yes, sir."

"Number two: you spend your free time with your squad. Is *that* clear?"

"Yes, sir."

"Number three: I'm going to be on your tail night and day. No more mollycoddling. You're my nephew, you're a Peña—I expect more of you, not less."

"Yes, sir."

"Every day I'm going to move you a little bit closer to the heart of what we do in this place. If you stay on the edge, the others won't trust you. I know the work is hard, I know it doesn't come naturally. You think I like this work?"

"No, sir."

"I hate this work. God knows how I hate this work. But it's my duty, and you do your duty or you are nothing but a traitor, you understand?"

"Yes, sir."

"Holy Mother, the things I've had to witness. They would make you sick just to hear about them. The war has forced this on us, the fucking Communists. I get no pleasure from what we do here. I just do my job, understand? And from now on, you will be one with the team. Otherwise, I'll send you back to Casarossa with my apologies. Or maybe not. Maybe I'll just shoot you myself."

"Yes, sir."

The Captain's anger seemed to ebb again. He took out his handkerchief and mopped his brow, and when he put it away his tone was softer.

"Listen, Victor, I have seen even some of the worst soldiers eventually shape up. I'm not giving up on you. First opening that comes available, I'll pull some strings and send you for training. Real training. They have a wonderful facility in Panama. Even better would be the United States. Fort Benning. That would be the best."

"The United States," Victor breathed with hope. "I could go to Fort Benning?"

"Possibly. But it's for soldiers, not cowards. Next detainee we bring in, I don't care who it is, you are going to get some hands-on experience, is that understood?"

"Yes, sir. Understood, sir."

TWO

THERE WAS NOT MUCH LEFT to identify the little school as a school. It sat like a red brick hat, neat and symmetrical, on the crest of a long, slow hill south of the city. Once there had been a small village around it, but when war came it had been necessary to remove the village. Faint rectangular outlines marked the places where the houses had been.

A perimeter of sandbags and barbed wire surrounded the school, and a makeshift gun tower rose like a periscope from the southeast corner where the play-ground used to be. And yet, despite the barbed wire and the sandbags and the gun turret, Captain Peña some-times imagined he could hear the shrill voices of school-children playing in the yard. The sounds of peace.

The walk was helping him calm down after yelling at his nephew. Now, as he climbed back up the hill, the only sounds were the lowing of cows and the stutter of gunfire from the nearby practice range. Captain Peña always took a walk after lunch, otherwise he had a tendency to be sleepy and then he would have trouble concentrating on the reports he had to read and write. He certainly couldn't afford to relax, not with the kind of men he was forced to work with.

A cow came right up to the fence at the edge of the road and looked at him with mournful eyes. The little school was a tranquil spot, all in all, and he hoped that one day it would be returned to its former purpose. Then again, it was war, and war changes everything and everyone. His peacetime career had been going so well— so had his war, until the Sumpul campaign. It was because of the Sumpul campaign that he was posted at the little school.

He came to the back step, where a young recruit was unloading a delivery.

"Did you bring my chocolate milk?"

"Yes, sir. Right here, sir."

The driver handed him a squat brown bottle and went back to unloading. He was maybe sixteen, his uniform drifting loosely around his neck and shoulders. Another soldier, no older, stood guard at the back of the truck. They were from the garrison down the road, the regular army. Aside from providing twenty-four-hour sentries for the barbwire perimeter, these deliveries were their only connection to the little school. An army of children, the Captain thought as he went inside. How can we win a war with an army of children?

"Ha! The Captain got his milk, I see," Tito said without looking up. Four of the squad were playing poker at the kitchen table. There was a game every lunch hour. The kitchen was the only room in the school that resembled what it had been before the war. "Some pull he must have to swing luxuries like chocolate milk."

"It's not a luxury. I have an ulcer from working with no-good bumpkins like you, sergeant."

"Give me two," Tito said to Lopez.

Lopez was the biggest man at the table, a perfect cube of muscle whose hands looked small and prim holding the cards. He flicked two cards at the sergeant. "Two for the bumpkin."

"Call me that again, you'll end up playing Submarine. Yunques, bring me a raincoat. Private Lopez wants to play Submarine."

The Captain sighed. It was terrible discipline, but that was one of the benefits they promised men they picked for squads like this—no uniforms, a more relaxed atmosphere. It's not like any other assignment in the army, they were told, you'll be joining a *team,* you'll be part of an elite unit, part of the advance guard.

It remained to be seen whether his nephew would ever be a part of this team. Victor was the son of the Captain's dead brother, and utterly without social sense. His brother had been a bit like that too; they had never been as close as he would have liked. When his brother had died of cancer—it was ten years ago now—he had sent money to Victor's mother every once in a while to help out, at least until Victor finished high school. His mother had died a few years ago, but by then the boy had been old enough to look after himself.

Or so the Captain had thought. He was damned if he was going to see a Peña executed for cowardice. He had to think of the family name. Shot before a firing squad? No, no. Captain Peña was honour bound to try his best for his nephew, even though everything the young man said or did seemed guaranteed to alienate the others. Too quiet, too polite, and always with his face in a book, as if he were still a student. Except for Sergeant Tito, none of the other men was even able to read, although, curiously, they had no trouble distinguishing one playing card from another.

The Captain missed the regular army, the fellowship of officers, people from his own class, but he lingered for a while, watching these coarse men finish their hand. Tito, at forty, was the oldest; the others were in their early twenties, not children at least. He sighed and looked out the window. It was barred like all the others—those that had not been bricked up—but this was the only room with a view of the hills. The cows had folded themselves up in a patch of sun.

Peacetime. In peacetime his nephew might have made something of himself, perhaps started a small business, married, and raised a few children. In peacetime no one would have discovered what a weakling he was, what an embarrassment. War shone a pitiless light on a man's character, and what was revealed was seldom flattering. Still, he didn't want to give up on the young man.

Lopez cursed under his breath. The sergeant charac-
teristically was holding his cards close. Discretion. Yes,
discretion was an important character trait. Loyalty,
patriotism and the unquestioning carrying out of every
order—these were crucial. Literacy was not even on
the list.

"You have ten minutes, my children. Lunch is over in
ten minutes."

"Who's on deck?"

"Unless I am mistaken, there is more to learn from
Labredo."

"Labredo? Labredo's a goner."

"Exactly why I want to hear from him."

Labredo had no information, the Captain knew, but it
was important for the men to believe they were hot on
the trail of priceless intelligence—the stray, half-forgotten
fact that might thwart a terrorist attack or save a campaign. They had to believe they were saving lives.

Lopez folded his cards. "Any bets Labredo makes it
past five o'clock?"

"You're not going to get any takers on that one, Lopez."

"Three o'clock, then. That's only two hours. He might
make it two hours."

"Labredo's a goner."

"Okay," said Lopez, "so let's make bets on his last
words. Fifty centivos he says *Oh, God.*"

The others laughed.

"*Oh, please. Oh, no. Oh, God . . .* It's got to be one of
those, right? That's pretty good odds."

"There's no point betting on things you can make happen," Tito pointed out.

"What do you mean? You can't know for sure something like a man's last words."

"If I feel like it, I can guarantee what the guy's last words are going to be. *Gua-ran-tee.*" Tito stabbed the table with his forefinger at each syllable.

"Oh, big shot here." Lopez leaned forward on his elbows. "What can you guarantee?"

"Fifty centivos his last words are *Please kill me.*"

"Exactly this? *Please kill me* exactly?"

"I don't know about exactly. *Please kill me* more or less."

"Oh, well, more or less. Nobody bets on more or less."

"Shut up now. That's enough."

All four men looked over at the Captain, who glared at them from beside the window.

"Where is your dignity?" he asked them, putting an edge into his voice. "Where is your self-respect? You think you're on some junior baseball team? This is not a sport we're involved in. This is not a game. Listen to me. Every time you are tempted to think we are playing a game, you remember. Remember that somewhere out there"—the Captain gestured toward the fields, the hills—"somewhere out there, your enemy is calling this exactly what it is. He is calling this *war.* And someday, when you are scouting some godforsaken barrio, or running half blind into some snake-infested village, or even driving down a halfway decent road— someday, when you are ambushed in your shiny little

Jeep—you will meet this man, my children. And he will kill you."

The Captain crossed the room to the door, and the four pairs of brown eyes followed him.

"It's one o'clock," he said. "Bring in Labredo."

THREE

ONLY TWO MONTHS PREVIOUSLY, Victor had been *in* a jail rather than guarding one. Being from a military family and having a high school diploma had made him prime officer material when he enlisted. And as Lieutenant Peña, he had several good months under his belt, running supplies along a coastal route considered only medium risk. Then one night, in a stunningly swift and brutal raid, the guerrillas slaughtered more than half the men in his command.

His sergeant had turned to yell something when his head exploded. Blood and brain matter blew into Victor's face. He fell choking into a pit slick with blood, firing blindly into the trees, and surely would have been killed with all his men had it not been for the purely accidental arrival of a helicopter gunship thrown off course by faulty electronics. The pilot had plucked Victor and his remaining men to safety.

Victor had posted three guards, the right number by the book, but "clearly insufficient for conditions," his superiors decided. Thus Lieutenant Peña was busted down to corporal. And that was not the end of his humiliation.

That night, that raid, undid him. Terror—at least in the field—became his mode of existence. The mere sound of automatic gunfire made him want to cry. And when, six months later, it came time to overrun a northern village suspected of harbouring rebels, Victor managed to charge smack into a guy wire, and spent the rest of the manoeuvre in a sheltering ditch, bleeding from a scalp wound. The resulting court martial sentenced him to death by firing squad.

His cell in the military jail had been much better than those in the little school, and he had not been abused by anyone. No, his torment had been simply to count down the hours to his certain death. After his sentence was pronounced, he had ten days to appeal, which was a joke, because in wartime there was no court of appeal. Victor wanted desperately to sleep through those ten days, but found he could not manage more than three or four hours a night, and even those were racked by savage dreams. His waking hours were consumed by an endless inner movie, rich with close-ups, of his own execution.

He had heard stories about firing squads. The worst was that all five men, none wanting to be the one to fire a lethal shot, would aim slightly away from the heart. The result, in more than one case, was that they blew off the condemned man's arms.

Then, one damp, grey afternoon, his uncle, Captain
Peña, had appeared before him like an angel of deliverance.

"You remember me, little Victor?"

"I remember you," Victor said, staring at his uncle,
who stood before him with a cowed-looking guard.
"But you're dead, I thought. They said you were killed
in San Vicente."

"So I was, as far as the press is concerned. That was
just public relations. They had to lower my profile, so to
speak, after all the noise about Sumpul."

The Sumpul River had been the site of a massacre.
Refugees had been driven by the Captain and his men
toward the border with Honduras. The Honduran army
had swept down with American helicopters and the
refugees had been caught between the two forces. The
army called it a great victory, announcing the death of
six hundred rebels. But the American ambassador had
made noises of discomfort when the bodies of women
and children continued to wash up on the shores for
weeks afterwards.

"Well, it looks like they're going to kill me, uncle."

"Lucky for you I came back from the dead. Casarossa
said he wouldn't protest if I removed you from his
command and made you disappear. You're the family
shame, Victor. A blot on the name of Peña. But if you're
not ready to die just yet, you can come and work for me.
One ghost working for another, eh?"

"You mean they're not going to shoot me?"

"You're coming with me—unless, of course, you'd rather die."

Which was how Victor came to find himself cleaning up after the high-pressure interrogation of Labredo. He had asked about the howls of agony issuing from that room shortly after his arrival at the little school. He was informed that there was no torture, only high-pressure interrogation.

In his brief tenure in the army, Victor had seen his share of gore. Even before the ambush that had killed his men, there had been the mopping-up operations, sudden descents on villages and outposts where he had seen dead bodies and parts of bodies dangling from tree branches, heads still in their helmets gazing at the sky with empty sockets. He had seen mothers weeping over their dead children, the innards hanging out of the little corpses like torn curtains. He had seen soldiers with the tops of their heads blown off, bodies hidden under heaving coverlets of flies and maggots. These sights Victor got used to. He would have gone mad in the first week otherwise.

And then his sergeant's brains had blown into his face.

He entered the former classroom with a mop and bucket and a few rags. He nearly choked on the smell of shit. He set down the bucket of soapy water and stared at the pool of blood congealing on the floor. It flowed out from a chair in the corner, colours fanning outward from bright crimson in the middle to rust brown at the fringes. The edges looked like a map of El Salvador's coastline.

He swung his mop in wide, rhythmic circles as if he were a brain-damaged person who had learned to perform this one function and nothing else. He tried to order his brain not to focus on the elements in his field of vision, and not to put diverse elements together to make up a whole. He did not want to see the whole.

Tools were laid out on a table by the bricked-up window, simple household items: a hammer, a pair of pliers, a roll of tape. He tried not to connect the hammer or the pliers—both darkened with blood—to the screams he had heard that afternoon. And the teeth on the floor. The clumps of hair. He tried to see these bits of human as inanimate objects only, unconnected to each other, unconnected to the hammer and the pliers. I am a janitor, he told himself. At this moment I am a soldier under orders to clean up a mess. That's all. I am not a philosopher, I am not a hero, I am no one's saviour.

Certainly he was not poor Labredo's saviour. Indeed, Sergeant Tito had ordered him to lead Labredo from the cells to this very room, the old man unresisting as a lamb. Now, Victor found one of Labredo's eyeballs impaled on a yellow pencil, propped on a corner of the desk like a drumstick.

He kept trying not to put everything together. But as he mopped under the desk, he found Labredo's other eyeball staring up at him in astonishment.

I led him here, Victor said to himself. I opened his cell and I led Labredo trembling, hardly able to walk, to an indescribable death.

He had brought Labredo, blindfolded—the prisoners were always blindfolded—out of his cell, the old man clinging to him as if he were his son. Victor had seen in his file that Labredo was not really an old man, he was only fifty-seven, but he had been in the little school for two months, and the photograph stapled to his dossier showed that he had looked very different when he had arrived.

After Victor had delivered Labredo into Sergeant Tito's hands, there had not been much noise the first half-hour, just the usual shouts and his uncle's quieter voice. Then his uncle had come out, grim-faced, and disappeared into his office. That was when the screams had started. Like a baby's cry, the human scream is meant to provoke sympathy and bring help. In the little school it brought laughter.

Victor hadn't had the courage to intervene, or even to run. He feared the bullet in the back. He feared being wounded, maimed or paralyzed; he feared capture. He feared what Tito would do to him. He feared his own screams. And so he had sat with his hands folded on the table in front of him and tried to breathe normally. The Captain had forbidden him to read, but he could not have read anyway. Labredo was begging the soldiers to kill him.

Victor had tried to concentrate on his surroundings. The guardroom was elongated, and there were holes along one wall. He had thought they were bullet holes, but that made no sense, not on this inner wall, and now he realized that what he was sitting in had been the cloakroom at the back of a classroom. The holes were where the hooks had been.

He counted the tiles on the floor, twenty-eight long, eight and a half wide. They alternated black and white, and if you looked at them quickly, they flashed in the corners of your eyes. On his left there was a large corkboard where the squad's schedule for the week was pinned, along with various notices, some of them yellowing with age. "General Emilio Garcia will be speaking Friday night on the relationship of the army to the community in the auditorium at the Central Business Association." General Garcia was long dead, his helicopter blown out of the sky two years ago by a remote-control bomb. A significant victory for the rebels.

The screams had stopped, but the muffled cries and continuing shouts indicated that Labredo's mouth had been taped shut. Even the toughest soldiers could bear only so many screams.

Half an hour later the door had banged open and the soldiers' voices billowed up the hall.

"Man, that son of a bitch was hard to kill."

"You owe me fifty centivos, Lopez."

"Bullshit. You taped the fucker's mouth shut. How do you know what his last words were?"

"He was begging us to kill him."

"Doesn't count. You gagged the little faggot."

"Peña," Tito shouted, "open up! Labredo's going back to his cell for a little snooze."

Victor sprang up and opened the door to the cells,

and Tito, Lopez and Yunques carried Labredo past him. He had a glimpse of the pulped, bloody face, the blood-soaked trousers and then the pale bare feet waving in the air.

"Clean up this faggot's mess," Tito grunted as they sidled past. "I want to see my face in that floor."

"Yes, sergeant."

"Lopez will take the guardroom. I want to see my face, understand?"

That night, they drove the Grand Cherokee through town to El Playón. There was no need for a blackout in San Salvador; it was well defended and the rebels had no planes, no helicopters. At the crosswalks, pedestrians glanced at the tinted windows and looked away, or crossed the street. The Cherokees were unmarked, but everyone knew they belonged to the security services. The vehicles intoxicated the soldiers inside as if they had been drinking.

"Look at that bitch," Yunques said, breathing garlic across Victor's face. He was pointing to a woman who backed away from the Jeep. "I think she's going to shit herself. You think that's really a baby she's carrying?"

"Why? You think she's carrying a bomb?"

"You never know."

"You just want to fuck her, Yunques. I know you."

"No, I don't. I want to fuck that little baby."

"He wants to fuck the baby up the ass. Fucking Yunques."

"I don't want to fuck it up the ass. I'm no pervert."

Their laughing filled the truck, and Victor had a vision of the laughter as heaps of garbage—bags of sour garbage bursting inside the truck.

"Hey, Labredo!" Tito called. "How you doing back there, baby?"

"Labredo's pissed off with you, man. He ain't going to talk to you no more."

Lopez put on a little voice, "Hey, somebody turn on the lights. I can't see a thing," and more laughter filled the truck.

"Man," Yunques said again, "that son of a bitch was hard to kill."

"I can't believe you took his eyes out before you finished him off. You got to *show* them what you're doing. That's the only way they get the fucking point. Eyes you always take last."

"I tried to put one back. Fucker wouldn't fit back in his head."

"Peña," Tito said when the laughter died down, "you're pretty quiet back there. You okay?"

"I'm okay, sergeant."

"You sure? No complaints?"

"No complaints at all, sergeant."

"You got any complaints, I want to hear them. Don't go yapping to your uncle, or I will personally roast your ass."

"No complaints, sergeant. I'm just fine."

"How you like the vehicle?"

"What? Oh, very nice. I used to daydream about owning one of these someday."

"Stick with this unit, baby, one day you'll own the fleet."

Even his uncle was besotted with the Cherokees. The day they had driven away from the military jail toward what Victor thought would be freedom, the Captain had slapped the steering wheel and said, "How do you like this machine?"

"It's beautiful," Victor had replied, and meant it. You didn't see a lot of new cars in El Salvador, let alone a fully loaded Cherokee smelling of new carpet and vinyl. And the tinted windows had the glamour—and anonymity—of sunglasses.

"Courtesy of the United States," his uncle went on. "They gave us a hundred of them. You believe that?"

"It's very generous."

"Fuck generous. They give us the money to *buy* the trucks. It's like they're handing it right to the Chrysler Corporation. You and me, little Victor, we're keeping those North Americans employed in Detroit."

Now Lopez was craning his neck in the back seat to look at a movie marquee. "Hey, anybody want to see a movie later?"

"Fuck that, Lopez. I'm tired."

"Fucking Clint Eastwood, man!" The movie was ancient. The picture showed Clint Eastwood with a big gun and Shirley MacLaine in a nun's habit.

"You think you're tired? Look at Labredo."

They had to stop as the few people coming out of the cinema crossed the street. The tinted glass formed grey halos round the street lights.

"Why can't they show those movies in Spanish?" Lopez wanted to know. "What do they think we are, fucking diplomats?"

"Yeah. Fucking faggot diplomats."

Tito gunned the motor and nearly ran down an old man who was slow to get out of his way. The man's cap fell off, but he recognized the Cherokee as a security vehicle and was too frightened to pick it up.

They drove in silence until Tito turned onto the road that curled up the hillside to El Playón.

"Why do we have to come here?" Lopez groaned. "Why can't we go to Diablo?"

"Diablo's for the live ones," Tito said. "Labredo is extremely dead. Anyway, what difference does it make?"

"This place stinks, that's all. Diablo at least you get some fresh air. This place, man, the smell is disgusting."

Yunques nudged Victor. "You want to cut off his thing?"

"What?"

"Labredo. You want to cut off his thing?"

"Why do you want to do that? The man is dead."

"Hey, sarge. Peña wants to know why we would cut off the faggot's *thing*."

"So tell him," Tito said.

Yunques breathed garlic over Victor again as he spoke. "We shove that little thing in their mouths so people get the message. You understand? People got to get the message. You don't join no guerrillas, you don't protest, you don't strike, you don't open your mouth against your country. You open your mouth, we shove your dick in it. Got it?"

"Got it."

"Good," Yunques said. "Come on, kids. Let's take out the trash."

The landscape before them rippled with black volcanic hills. Tito left the Cherokee's headlights on bright; they rimmed the hills with silver. Before the war, the area had been a tourist attraction. Victor remembered visiting it as a child. The bald black hills were a striking sight against a blue sky, and there was a hot spring somewhere. But tourists didn't come to El Playón anymore. In daytime the circling buzzards could be seen for miles.

"Pull your kerchief up, man. You'll need it."

Yunques pulled his own neckerchief up over his face like a bandit. Victor did the same.

Lopez lifted Labredo by the arms, Yunques and Victor each took a leg. Sergeant Tito led the way with a powerful flashlight. Steam rose into the beam in lush plumes.

"Fuck this. I can't see a thing."

Victor stepped on something soft, which suddenly gave way beneath his foot with a snap. Someone's rib cage. "Oh, Jesus."

"Yeah, man. The smell is something."

"No, I stepped on somebody."

"Well, watch where you step. You'll stink up the car. Over this way."

They swung east, and the lights of the city were flung out below them.

Lopez let go, and Labredo's head hit a rock with a thud.

"Oh, man, the smell. Let's get out of here."

The other two let go and they turned back toward the truck. The smell finally flipped Victor's stomach right over, and he had to yank his kerchief out of the way to vomit.

"Thanks a lot, Peña. Nice touch."

"He can't help it," Lopez said. "First time I was out here, I did the same thing."

They headed back to the car, Victor watching where he stepped the whole time.

As Tito backed it up, the lights caught on a bleached face here, an outflung arm there. Wisps of steam clung to the rocks like hair.

"I'm sorry I got sick," Victor said hoarsely. "The smell . . ."

"You'll get used to it," Yunques said. "Doesn't take long."

"You get used to everything," Lopez said. "It's incredible what you get used to."

Next morning, his uncle found him in the guardroom. "Not reading for once."

"No, sir."

"Good. You won't have any time for books now. They're bringing someone in. And this one you're going to work on with the others. You're one of the team, understand?"

"Yes, sir."

"You're either with us or you're with them, understand?"

"Yes, sir. I understand."

FOUR

SHE WAS BLINDFOLDED, of course, they were always blindfolded. She stood just inside the door, her hands behind her back. She was a skinny woman, taller than Victor, with thin dark hair that hung straight to her shoulders. A large watch with an expandable band hung loosely about one wrist. She was wearing jeans and a tank top. It was cool in the office and there were goose-bumps on her arms.

"First thing you have to learn is intake procedure." Captain Peña waved a sheaf of forms at Victor. "Whoever picked her up will fill out a report, but you want to take it down first-hand from the—"

"I want to know what are the charges," the woman said. She had a harsh voice with a catch in it, the voice of a crow.

Captain Peña looked up at her with an appraising glance. "I'll get to you in just a moment," he said politely, then turned once more to Victor. "But you still want to take down the prisoner's version of events, because—"

"You have no right to keep me here. I want to speak to someone in charge."

"Young lady, you are going about this the wrong way entirely. Two minutes have not gone by and already you are antagonizing me."

"Why should you be antagonized by a request for just treatment under the law?"

Victor was surprised by her boldness. None of the other prisoners protested this way. Most never spoke at all; to do so was to risk a rifle butt in the ribs.

"Perhaps you don't realize," the Captain said gently. "Under Decree 107 you can be detained up to ten days without charges. And you should also know that I run this place."

"I want to speak to your superior officer. You think this is how law-abiding citizens are to be treated?" Being blindfolded, she addressed her cawing to a space between Victor and his uncle.

"Miss, you will meet the General soon enough," Captain Peña said. "Please be patient. Actually," he said, turning to Victor, "I've already given you the wrong impression. Normally I don't have any conversation with a prisoner on intake. It threw me off, her being a woman."

He got up from his desk and went over to the woman. He took hold of her elbow. "Excuse me," he said. "You're right in the doorway here, could you just move over a little bit?"

The woman moved awkwardly a pace or two, her back against the wall. "I would like to speak to a lawyer. I have the right to representation."

"Could you just move your left foot, please? You know the 'at ease' position? I want you to stand at ease."

The Captain tapped the instep of her left foot with his army boot. She was wearing grubby tennis shoes with red trim. She moved her foot aside so that her feet were about two feet apart.

"Thank you," said Captain Peña, then kicked her full force between the legs. She fell to her knees and curled up as if she had taken a bullet.

Fear slipped into Victor's bloodstream like acid.

"The official form of greeting," his uncle said. "Man, woman, doesn't matter. You have to let them know right away that here the rules do not apply. This is their welcome to a different universe, where mercy does not exist. You have a problem with that, soldier, you go back and explain to Casarossa." He shouted for a guard, and Lopez came in. "Put her in a cell, we'll talk to her later."

Lopez pulled her roughly to her feet. She was not able to stand upright. She was still gulping for air. Victor suddenly understood another reason for the blindfold: tears would not show.

"Hold it," the Captain said.

Lopez paused at the door, and Captain Peña reached for the woman's arm and pulled a watch from her wrist.

"It has a metal band," he said to Victor. "We don't want her cutting anything." When the door had closed, the

Captain said, "We'll give her three days to think about things. We will keep her a little hungry, we will keep her a little cold, and, most important of all, we will keep her a little tired. This will be your responsibility. Three days from now, I want her nerves to be screaming."

"What has she done? She doesn't look like a terrorist."

"You think terrorists look like terrorists? Obviously, the first thing they learn is how to be inconspicuous. Mother of God, if we went by appearances, we'd never catch anybody."

"Captain, I don't think I'm ready for this."

"Not ready? You want to tell Casarossa you're not ready, I'll take you over there myself. We are interrogating rebels here—socialist pigs who want to destroy everything we believe in. If you are not ready for that, then as far as I'm concerned you *deserve* to die."

"But, Captain . . . she's a woman."

"She is not a woman, she is a terrorist. If we do our job right and get some information out of her, we will save lives. And if you do *your* job right, then by the time we interrogate her we won't have to use that much pressure. You will save her a lot of pain."

"First day, you don't feed her nothing," Lopez told him. The Captain had instructed Lopez to show Victor the ropes, which seemed to boost the big man's mood. He was friendlier to Victor than anyone had been since his arrival. "You don't feed her nothing, understand? You don't take her to the latrine, you don't give her no bucket. Nothing.

If she speaks, you scream at her to shut up. You never talk, never use your normal voice, always scream. And never use their name, always call them something bad: pig, cunt, faggot, whore—doesn't matter. They have to learn exactly what they're worth. I'll be back in a second."

Lopez went out and Victor remained at the little table facing the corridor of cells. There were eight prisoners in the first cell, ten in the second, and the third, a tiny little chamber hardly six feet square, held only the woman. Across from this there was a solitary cell containing a man named Perez. There was not a sound from any of them.

Victor had not yet recovered from the shock of seeing his uncle kick the woman, hard enough to break the pubic bone you would have thought. He could never have imagined his uncle—so upright, so correct— kicking a woman.

He stood up and yelled, "Blindfold!" The guards always did this, so that any prisoner whose blindfold had slipped could readjust it. And prisoners were anxious to keep the blindfolds in place; to see a guard's face was certain death.

Victor peered into the first cell, where the prisoners were laid out like sardines, head to feet, on the mattresses on the floor. None of them stirred. The second cell was the same, although at the sound of the peephole opening, one of them moaned for the latrine.

She was curled up on the bed, holding her abdomen. At the sound of the grate she moved her head slightly, but did not speak.

"Soldier!" This was Lopez yelling for him. Guards never called each other by name in front of prisoners. Victor shut the peephole and went back to the table. Lopez was there with a water bucket. "What's she doing?"

"Nothing. Lying down."

"Good. Go soak her with this."

Victor took the bucket without a word. Ice cubes clicked against metal.

"I'll open the door, you toss it and get out."

They went down the corridor and Lopez opened the door.

The woman sat up at the sound and waited, breathing through her mouth. Victor hurled the water at her and it caught her right in the chest, completely soaking her shirt, her jeans and the mattress she sat on. She jumped up with a cry and stood gasping.

"Come on, soldier. Don't hang around."

Lopez locked the door and Victor followed him back to the guardroom.

"Good shot, man."

His uncle was away for the afternoon, so Victor felt safe reading. He finished the Steinbeck and moved on to a James Bond story. He didn't like it, but kept reading to keep his mind off what he had done. Soaking the woman with ice water. Well, it wasn't torture, he supposed, but he had never done anything mean to a woman in his life. His father and mother had taught him to stand up when a woman entered the room, to offer his seat to a woman on the bus. And now he was expected to soak this prisoner again before he went off duty.

At six, Lopez came from the kitchen with a cart full of the evening meal. The prisoners got beans and tortillas, or beans and bread, always cold. Never anything else, never anything hot.

They passed the food through the slots of cells one and two, and then Lopez said, "Perez don't get nothing tonight. But we'll mix up something special for the new bitch." He went out to the kitchen and came back with a half-pound container of salt. He handed it to Victor. "Go ahead, man. Pour it on."

Victor poured a few tablespoons into the beans.

"Not like that, man. You got to really pour it on!" Lopez grabbed his wrist and twisted so that salt poured onto the plate in a white heap. "Stir it, man. Mix it in there!"

Victor stirred the mixture until it was thick as plaster. He delivered it to the cell and came back without waiting to see if she ate it.

"We don't want them to say we don't feed them."

"What about Perez?"

"Take him something if you want, he won't eat it. The sergeant was playing dentist with him this afternoon."

As if hearing his name, Sergeant Tito arrived for a surprise inspection.

"Blindfold!" He strode right past the guardroom to the cells. He glanced in one after another, not pausing for more than three seconds before any of the doors. "Soldier! Outside!"

Victor followed his sergeant out to the yard. Tito screamed at him. "Your orders are to keep that woman wet at all times. Ice water every two hours. Can you explain why she is dry?" Before Victor could answer, Tito slapped the side of his head. "You going to make up your own rules now? Who do you think you are?" Again the open hand connected with his ear.

Victor's head was ringing. "No one told me every two hours. I was going to do it again later."

"You want to take a swim in the tank, Peña?"

"No, sergeant."

"You want to play a little Submarine?"

"No, sergeant."

"Then get a bucket and soak that bitch right now. You soak her and you keep her soaked. If that bitch gets so much as thirty seconds of sleep, I'll cut your prick off, you hear me?"

Victor fetched a bucket of water. The woman backed toward the wall. He didn't hesitate this time. He threw the water at her, and she shrank from him but made no sound.

His nights in the barracks were miserable. The other members of the squad had their own apartments in the city. That was part of the privilege of working for the squad, you didn't have to live in barracks, you got to have your own place. But Victor was still on probation. For now, he lived in a tiny room at one end of the little school. It had five sets of iron bunk beds—all, except for his, with mattresses rolled up at one end.

He read late that night; books were the only thing that kept him sane. On his last day off he had ventured into the city and bought a stack of ten American novels from a used-book store. The Hemingway disappointed him because it was set in Europe, not North America, and Faulkner was too difficult. Victor finally settled on a detective novel, and it absorbed him completely. He didn't have to look up too much vocabulary, and it was set in New York. The story took him from the luxurious apartments on Fifth Avenue to the sweatshops of Chinatown.

When he awoke the next morning, he thought there was a red dog lying on his chest. Try as he might to shift it, the dog would not get off. As his mind cleared, he realized the weight on his chest was fear.

He thought of the new woman prisoner. If *he* felt isolated and fearful, how must *she* feel? She would not have slept. She would have been too cold, too wet, too hungry. He had soaked her thoroughly before he went off duty, and when Yunques relieved him, he had added his own bucket right away. "Tits are too small," he said with a grimace. Yunques was always saying tough things, but sometimes Victor wondered if he wasn't putting on a show of bravado. Perhaps Sergeant Tito could be that carelessly cruel, but Victor wondered about Yunques and Lopez. Maybe under the macho talk they were just as scared as he was.

———

"Please. I want to see a lawyer," the woman said. Victor had just thrown a full bucket of ice water on her, and rivulets streamed down her face. "I have done nothing wrong. I was simply taking food to the church basement."

Victor stood in the door of her cell, breathing hard. Prisoners were supposed to be struck whenever they spoke. He locked the cell door and went back to the guardroom.

She called after him in her unpleasant voice: "And I would like some food, please."

"Special treat for the new bitch," Lopez said. "Take a look at this." He opened the lid of a small cardboard box, revealing the cockroaches.

"You going to put them in her cell?"

"Her cell?" Lopez looked truly puzzled. "Why would we put them in her cell?"

"For a joke?"

"We are not joking here, soldier. You should've figured that out by now."

"I'm sorry. I'll get the hang of things, I'm sure."

"Put these in her food and serve it to her."

Victor did as he was told.

"Well?" Lopez said when he came back. "How'd the bitch like it?"

"She felt the bugs," Victor said. "Then she just put the plate on the floor and lay down again."

"Really? She didn't cry or nothing?"

"No."

"You know, I think she may be a real hard-ass terrorist, this one. Most women scream like a motherfucker when we give them the bug dinner."

"That doesn't make her a terrorist."

"I'll bet you, Peña. She's too hard for a civilian."

The woman didn't touch any food they brought her that day. When Victor threw the bucket of water at her, she did not cry out, even though he aimed it well to make sure she was good and soaked in case Tito should stick his ugly head in again.

The next day, she ate a plate of heavily salted beans and asked several times for water, but no water was brought to her. Later, when Victor checked on her through the peephole, he saw her sucking water out of her shirt, the way an infant sucks a beloved blanket.

Sergeant Tito came for her that afternoon. "Bring her out, soldier. Don't tell her nothing what's going on. She will learn soon enough."

"Blindfold!"

Lopez unlocked the cell door and Victor went in for the woman. She was crouched against the wall, her arms curled up in front of her, expecting a soaking.

Victor took hold of her elbow and she yanked it away. He jerked harder.

"Where are you taking me?"

"You're going to have a chat with the General," Lopez said. "That's what you wanted, right?"

Victor led her along the corridor.

"Where is the General?" she demanded as soon as she was brought into the interrogation room.

Tito and the Captain were sitting at a small table. Yunques was not around, and Tito motioned for Victor to stand by the wall.

"Have a seat, please," said the Captain. "What is your name, please?"

"Maria Sanchez."

"You don't want to tell me your name?"

"I just told you my name. Maria Sanchez."

"That is a lie. But I will tell you *my* name." The Captain got up and leaned down beside her ear. Even though his voice was barely above a whisper, she flinched when he spoke. "My name," he said, "is God."

FIVE

ONCE, WHEN VICTOR was in high school, he had been caught smoking on school property. The vice-principal, a prematurely bald and angry man, had taken him to the office and offered him a choice: Victor could take a two-week suspension or the strap.

"There is the telephone, Peña." The bald head gleamed for an instant as he nodded at the terrifying instrument. "Call your father and explain to him why you will be missing class for the next two weeks. Tell him why you will miss the term review just as your exams are approaching—because you had to have a cigarette on school property, even though you are well aware of the rules. Go on now, Peña, you call the Major and ask him what to do."

The prospect of such a conversation with his father was a brick wall. Take a two-week suspension? The Major would beat him about the head. He would make him suffer for a year.

"I will take the strap, sir," Victor had said. It couldn't be worse than his father's fists. Many boys got the strap, and all of them said it didn't hurt, they didn't cry.

"Very good, Peña. Bend over the desk and take hold of the far edges."

Victor bent over, feeling horribly exposed even though his trousers had not been lowered. He caught a glimpse of the strap as the vice-principal took it down from the shelf. It was about fifteen inches long, and much thicker than he expected—a quarter-inch of leather. He gripped the far side of the desk and tried to fix his mind on the bookshelves that faced him. There were no book titles to read, however, just large binders—probably full of dossiers on delinquent students like himself.

He looked back over his shoulder and caught a glimpse of the vice-principal leaning back, his wind-up for the first blow. There was a whistling sound and then the smack of leather on flesh. Victor shrieked. The strap felt like a patch of fire across his skin, and tears sprang into his eyes.

The strap whistled again, and again he shrieked. To his dismay, he now began to cry helplessly; great gasping sobs shook his body. He could not catch his breath, and the hot tears streamed down his cheeks. Deep inside, a voice spat the word, "Coward."

"Holy Mother, Peña." There was genuine puzzlement in the vice-principal's voice. "That's only two strokes. I don't know if you're faking or not."

Victor's voice was choked and unrecognizable.

"Nobody's ever screamed like that. I know you're a skinny runt, but really—try and control yourself. It can't hurt that much."

But Victor could not control himself. The vice-principal threw himself into the remaining eight blows, and rained them down so quickly that Victor scarcely had time to breathe before the next one landed. When the blows were done, he nearly passed out.

"Sit there until you catch your breath. Go on. Sit down and put your head between your knees. You look like you're about to faint."

Victor did as he was told, staring at the polished wooden floor. He had to breathe through his mouth, his sinuses were so clogged from crying.

"Really, Peña," the vice-principal said, not unkindly. "You frightened me." He opened a file and began to read. He did not speak again until Victor stood up. "Go into the washroom now and wash your face with cold water. I will tell no one what has happened here today."

Everyone will know anyway, Victor thought; his eyes were bloodshot, his cheeks puffy. When he quietly took his seat in history class, the other pupils glanced over at him, but no one said anything. Nor did anyone mention it to him when class was over, or in the following weeks. He could not tell if his classmates' silence was born of sympathy or contempt.

He had come that day to his first disillusionment. Until then he had cherished an unsupported conviction that he could be heroic under the right circumstances. In time of peril, he would risk his own life to save a woman or a child, he would brave flames or gunfire to help the helpless. But the vice-principal had shown him that Victor Peña was not the stuff of which heroes are made.

And now he was learning this lesson again—this time from a skinny woman with an unpleasant voice.

"My name is God," Captain Peña told her that first day. "I am the Lord of Life and Death. Whatever I say will happen, that is what will happen. If you cherish any illusions about this, abandon them now. In this place there are no rules except the rules I make. If I decide you should live, you will live; if I decide you should die, you will die. The sooner you understand this, the easier it will go with you."

"I want a lawyer," the woman said. Even green Victor could see this was the wrong tone to take with the Captain.

"There are no lawyers," he replied. "There are no laws. Now, what is your name?"

"My name is Maria Sanchez. Look at my birth certificate."

"Your birth certificate is a fake."

"No, it is not. I want to know why I have been brought here."

"You have been brought here as a suspected terrorist."

"For taking food to the church basement."

"Food for whom?"

"For children orphaned by the war."

"The children of terrorists, you mean. Sympathy for them is sympathy for terrorism."

"They are children, and they will starve unless we feed them."

"What is your name?"

"Maria Sanchez."

Captain Peña got up and stood beside her. He unzipped his fly, pulled out his penis, and pressed it against her cheek. The woman jerked her head aside.

"Tell us your name right now."

"Maria Sanchez. My name is Maria Sanchez."

There was a bed along one wall, a narrow cot with only the metal springs showing. A mattress was brought in. The woman was stripped and secured by wrists and ankles to the bed frame. Captain Peña lowered his trousers and lay down on top of her. She screamed obscenities at the ceiling and tried to bite him.

Yunques yanked her head back by the hair.

The Captain had trouble entering her. The woman screamed and screamed, and Victor tried to look anywhere but at the bed, at the pale buttocks heaving up and down. A series of grunts signalled the end and then the Captain climbed off.

The woman was crying now, cursing him through the tears.

"I hope you are taking the pill," he said matter-of-factly. "There are three more men here."

The woman's abdomen heaved. She let out a scream that tore into Victor like a machete.

"Tell us your name."

The woman could not have answered even if she had wanted to. She was beyond the reach of the Captain's words. He yelled at her several more times to reveal her name, but she only kept screaming.

Tito climbed on top of her.

She turned her head to the wall.

"Tell us your name and this will stop."

"You are scum. I will tell you nothing."

Yunques was next. It seemed to go on forever, the squeak of the springs and the cries she tried to suppress.

"What is your name?"

"Maria Sanchez. Please stop. Please don't do this anymore."

"It's very easy. Tell us your name and it will stop."

"I've told you my name. Maria Sanchez."

The Captain snapped his fingers at Victor. In their excitement, the others had forgotten he was there. Now they looked at him, and Victor knew there was no escape. To hesitate would be death: he would be taken out and shot, or they would drown him in that tank full of piss and shit—at best, he would be delivered to Casarossa and shot by firing squad. He unbuckled his trousers and lay on top of the woman.

Her skin was scorching. She smelt like a wet dog. Victor's penis was a tiny, fearful thing in his hand. He pretended to enter her. He humped up and down a few times. Then he groaned and climbed off.

If she revealed his fakery, he was dead.

But she did not. She cried behind her blindfold, and the small breasts quivered with each sob.

They raped her repeatedly over the next three days, Victor faking it each time, until they tired of her. By then she was becoming too swollen for them to enter.

"This is just the softening-up process," Captain Peña told Victor in his office. "We don't really expect them to talk during these preliminaries. It's just to break their spirit. If she was a man, we'd make him eat shit. Then, when we begin the real pressure, they will know who they are dealing with."

"But it's illegal, isn't it? I mean, it's rape, isn't it?"

"You saw what happened to Labredo. You think she would prefer the Labredo methods?"

"No. I'm just worried, you know, about the law."

"'In the defence of one's country, there is no such thing as a crime.' You know who said that?"

"The President?"

"Napoleon said that. The greatest warrior, the most enlightened ruler, who ever lived." His uncle lit a cigarette and exhaled the smoke luxuriously. "Look, I don't get any kick out of screwing this bitch. It's just a technique, like any other. You afraid she's going to tell someone?"

"I don't know. I guess so."

"She will tell no one. If she has a husband, he will disown her. If she does not have a husband and this gets out, she will never get one. I think you're making a fundamental confusion," his uncle said more softly.

"What is that, sir?"

"You are confusing what happens in here with our lives outside. Obviously, none of us is the kind of person who would do these things in the normal course of existence. It doesn't reflect on who you are as a person. War is a separate reality."

"Yes, sir."

"If you have any questions, Victor, ask me now. I am your uncle and I want you to understand."

"I do have one question, sir."

"Go ahead."

"Why are you so sure this woman is with the rebels?"

The Captain shrugged and exhaled a stream of smoke. "I'm not."

SIX

THE WOMAN PUT UP A STRUGGLE when they came for her each morning. She would curl up against the wall, she would kick out wildly, unseeing, but her attempts to evade them were hopeless. Lopez would simply punch her in the stomach, and then they would carry her, doubled over, along the hall to interrogation.

"So stupid," Lopez remarked. "You'd think she'd get the idea first time."

On the fourth day, the routine changed. Sergeant Tito came instead of Lopez. "Congratulations, bitch," he said. "The General's here to see you. You get to take a shower." She backed away from them as she always did. Tito seized her by the arm. "We can't have you going in there like this. You smell like shit."

The shower was in the soldiers' bathroom, just off the kitchen. They led her past the other cells, the woman moving in a hunched, head-down way that was new in her. Even so, she had the temerity to question them. "Which general is it? What is his name?"

"I'm not authorized to tell you his name," Tito said. "Maybe he'll tell you, if you ask politely."

"But he is in charge of the jails, this general? He interviews all the prisoners?"

"Yes, most of the prisoners get to have a chat with the General. I guarantee, he will be interested in your views."

"Do I get to speak to him alone?"

"We will be there the whole time. Why? You're not planning to tell him anything nasty about us, are you?"

"I will tell him the truth."

Tito jerked her shoulders so that she banged her forehead against the doorway. "Sorry," he said.

They took her into the bathroom and removed the thong that bound her thumbs together. Tito started the water.

"Can I take my blindfold off?"

"Not if you want to live. We'll be right here, watching you. Take your time. Get nice and clean. We don't want the General thinking we mistreat you."

For the next fifteen minutes, Tito sat at the kitchen table and drank a coffee, muttering over the sports section. Victor remained standing with his back to the bathroom doorway. When he finished his coffee, Tito got up and removed the woman's clothing from the floor where she had left it folded.

The water stopped running. "Is there a towel, please?"

"No towel," Tito snapped. "You don't need no towel."

She stood with her arms folded in front of her. She looked even skinnier in the shower, ribs showing beneath the tiny breasts. Even with the blindfold obscuring her expression, Victor saw she was trying to assess the situation. She squatted down and felt the floor where her clothes had been. The ugly voice dropped down a note. "May I have my clothes, please?"

"No point," Tito said. "The general will just have you take them off again. He will be checking you for marks of mistreatment. Cuffs." She turned around and Tito looped the thong around her thumbs and pulled it tight.

When they led her out into the hall, Yunques whistled.

"Shh," Tito hissed. "The General's here!"

"Oh, shit. Sorry, sergeant."

Captain Peña was waiting for them in the interrogation room, sitting at the little table like a customs official. There was a pad and a jar of pencils in front of the chair beside him. He motioned to Victor to sit there, then turned his attention to the woman. "We will be taking down a transcript of everything that is said here today. Please be seated and tell the General your name."

Tito led the woman to the chair and set her squarely in front of it. Naked and dripping water, she sat down. Victor noticed on the desk a piece of equipment he had not seen before, a black box the size of a tabletop radio with a pointed dial in the middle. Two black leads coiled out from it, and above the dial were two words in white script, *General Electric*.

"Will you tell the General your real name," the Captain said. "Don't give us the Maria Sanchez line again."

"Maria Sanchez happens to be my real name. I can't help it if it's a common name. General, are you here?" Blindly, she turned her head toward Victor. "General, these men have raped me every day since I've been here. For three days now. Every morning they rape me."

Tito shouted, "She's lying, General! Don't believe her!"

"Every morning they come for me, they hit me. They hit me and then drag me here and rape me. Please, won't you have a doctor examine me? He will see I have been raped." She choked on the words, struggling to get her breath.

This woman hides her fear better than I, Victor had thought more than once. But nothing is more expressive than the naked human body. Although the room was hot, the woman's small muscles shook as if exposed to icy winds. And with every breath, a deep quiver travelled through her in a wave.

"She's lying," Tito said again. "We are not animals here."

"Shh," Captain Peña said. "Quiet, sergeant. Let the prisoner speak."

"General—" She choked back tears to address Victor once more. "I swear to you I have done nothing wrong. I have broken no laws. I am not with the rebels. I don't know any rebels. I am not even political. I don't deserve to be treated like this. Nobody deserves to be treated like this."

Victor concentrated on writing her words down. It gave him an excuse to avoid her blind stare.

Lopez was about to say something. Captain Peña cut him off with a motion of his hand. There was a long pause, the only sound that of the woman's sobbing. Clear mucus dripped from her nose and she tried to sniff it back. "May I dry myself, please?"

"You may not. The General wants you nice and wet. Are you going to tell him your real name now?"

"Maria Sanchez. It's the only name I have."

"All right, Miss Sanchez. Have it your way. Shake hands with General Electric." The Captain gestured at Victor. "You do it. Sergeant, show him how."

The woman's hands were tied to the arms of the chair. Tito showed him the tube of conductive jelly, the electrodes with their little alligator clamps and duct tape. Then the sergeant grabbed the index finger of her left hand. "For fingers, just use the electrode. You tape it."

"Don't do it for him," said the Captain. "Let him do it. He has to learn."

The woman started to kick, and Lopez tied her feet to the chair legs.

Victor spread conductive jelly on the woman's bony finger. It was messy, his hands were shaking so badly. "Don't do this," the woman said. "Please do not do this."

"Shut up, whore." Tito slapped her hard across the head. "Do the other hand. Same finger."

When it was done, the Captain told Victor to sit down again. "All right, soldier. Watch where I put this dial. There is an art to it." He turned the dial to the number two.

The woman made a sound like nothing Victor had ever heard—a prolonged, unearthly howl.

The Captain shouted over her. "Don't give them any more than thirty seconds the first time. We want them still able to talk." He turned the dial back to zero and the woman slumped in her chair.

She's dead, Victor thought. But after a moment she started to breathe, inhaling with a sound like tearing fabric.

"You do it this time." The Captain slid the black box toward Victor. "Turn it a little higher. Around three." Victor turned the dial, and the Captain shouted again over the woman's howls: "Second time, you give them a little more. And a little longer. Forty-five seconds to a minute."

Victor turned the dial back to zero and the woman fell to one side—so heavily that both she and the chair tipped over.

Tito and Lopez set the prisoner upright again. "Goddamn," Tito said, "she's really out." He patted her cheeks—a strangely gentle thing to do, under the circumstances.

The Captain ordered Lopez to bring water. Lopez returned a moment later with two large bottles of Perrier water, as if he were making a joke. He shook one of the bottles and held his thumb over the opening, spraying the woman from head to foot.

"Makes it worse," the Captain explained. "The minerals are more conductive."

Lopez shook the bottle again and sprayed her until it was empty. When she was fully conscious again, the Captain turned on the machine. Every muscle in her body stood out like a rope, and once more she made that terrible sound.

"Third time, you really let them have it. Turn it up to four, maybe even five if they are strong enough. Give them maybe two minutes."

This time it took ten minutes to revive her. "Next session I will give her less and we will have the doctor on hand. It's always hard to judge first time with a prisoner. But I think today she will tell us her name."

I would have told them everything in the first minute, Victor thought.

"Take down whatever she says—it's important to keep a record."

Captain Peña stood over the woman. For the hundredth time, he asked her her name. But she was only capable of groaning now. "Mother of God, Mother of God . . ."

"It's entirely up to you how long it takes. We have all the time in the world, here."

The woman said something unintelligible.

"What's that? What did you say?"

"Decree," she managed. "Decree 107. Ten days only. Ten days, you have to let me go. It's the law."

The Captain looked at Tito, and the two of them laughed. After a moment's hesitation Lopez and Yunques joined in. Victor smiled as if he saw the joke too.

The Captain raised his hand for silence. "You really imagine we're just going to let you go? 'Oh, thank you very much, Ms. *Sanchez,* sorry to bother you'? Sorry, bitch. It doesn't work like that."

"You have only ten days. Ten days is the law." Somehow she had found her voice again.

"What is your name?"

"I will never tell you my name."

The Captain and Tito exchanged a glance. They'd both heard it. At last the woman had admitted she still had a name to reveal. Victor saw her mouth open after she had spoken, as if to suck the words back in again. It was her first mistake, and she knew she'd made it.

SEVEN

"I KNOW EXACTLY what it feels like," his uncle said.

They were driving up the winding street to his house in the Santa Ana area. It was a good neighbourhood; one could tell by the height of the walls surrounding each property. Some were as high as sixteen feet, composed of different layers of brick and stone, like geological strata. All were topped with razor wire.

His uncle had moved here only recently, after his convenient "death," and Victor couldn't imagine how he could afford it. The area was far too exclusive for most military men. In fact, Victor remembered an occasion as a child walking through this neighbourhood just out of curiosity, staring in wonder at the houses set like jewels at the end of their long driveways. There were no walls then, just the long drives and the palm trees and the houses that looked like palaces out of fairy stories. He could not believe that the little children playing in the yards were of the same flesh and blood as he, they looked so clean and pretty.

Then a Guardia patrol stopped him and told him to get the hell out—he did not belong there. He didn't even resent them for it, because he knew they were right.

"Yes," his uncle was saying, "I am personally familiar with the General's handshake."

"I'm astounded," Victor said. "You were actually tortured?"

"Of course I was not tortured. What we do at the little school is not torture. It's high-pressure interrogation. Torture is what they did to the martyrs—skinning them alive, cooking them, that kind of thing."

Victor did not see how this differed from the sufferings of Pedro Labredo. "Who interrogated you?"

"Some Guardia asshole. This was two governments ago. Before your time. They thought I was part of a coup conspiracy. I wasn't, unfortunately—I'd be a lot richer now if I had been. Anyway, this Guardia guy, he introduced me to the General, and let me tell you, it hurt like hell. You know what it feels like, Victor? It feels as if your flesh is splitting open. It feels as if your flesh is splitting open to the bone. You remember that little earthquake we had a few years back? That crack that opened up all along Ilopango Street?"

"I remember."

"That's how it feels. Like your flesh is splitting open. You stare at yourself afterwards—you look at your arms and legs, you feel your belly—and you're amazed that your flesh is still together over your bones. You can't believe you haven't split in pieces. There's no way you can keep silent. It rips the screams right out of your throat."

"God, Uncle. How did you stand it?"

"I couldn't stand it. I wanted only to die. If I had had *anything* to tell them, I would have told them: names, dates, locations, you name it. I would have given up my mother to stop that pain."

"But the Sanchez woman—she's been taking it for three days now. Surely if she had anything to give up, she would have done so by now."

His uncle shrugged. "Some guys, you can pull their teeth out one by one and they won't tell you a thing. Pull their hair out? Nothing. You break their fingers? Silence. Then one day, for a little variety, you force them to swallow a few turds. Suddenly they sing like a sparrow. Just a little shit! It's not even painful! Suddenly you can't shut them up." The Captain shook his head in wonder. "I am constantly amazed by human nature."

Captain Peña's house turned out to be a modest two-storey adobe, much smaller than its neighbours, hidden behind the highest walls on the crest of a hill. They were greeted at the side door by Victor's aunt, a slim woman in her mid-forties, slightly bent at the shoulders, as if weighed down with some old sorrow. Whatever grief this might have been, she had long ago learned to keep hidden behind a wide, reassuring smile.

"You are out of the infantry now, at least," she said to Victor when they were settled in the living room with tea and biscuits. She made no mention of his having recently been condemned to death. "I'm so glad for you. It's terrible what our soldiers have to endure out there." She gestured vaguely, as if "out there" encompassed every place on the far side of her lace curtains, as if once you got beyond the gleaming floors, and the smells of lemon oil and lavender, only chaos could be expected to reign.

"Yes," Victor said. "Lucky for me the Captain saw fit to rescue me."

"Couldn't have a blot on the Peña name, could we, my dear?" The Captain put an arm around his wife and pulled her close. "Old Iron Pants here wouldn't stand for it." He winked at Victor.

"Don't you call me that," said his wife with a weary laugh. "Iron Pants, really. Did you ever hear such a thing?"

"It's true. This little woman has more macho than our entire squad, I'm not kidding you. I have to watch what I do."

"Eduardo is always telling me that he's not as stern as everyone says he is," Mrs. Peña said. "But frankly, I have my doubts."

"He does run a tight outfit," Victor said with a smile. "Very disciplined."

"Really? He's quite a softie at home. Do you remember from when you visited us as a boy? Once he comes through that door—poof!—no discipline at all."

As if to demonstrate the point, Captain Peña's twin daughters, seven years old, came in with their nanny. At first, in the presence of a stranger, they were subdued and quiet. They were introduced and made solemn curtsies and smiled, showing matching gaps where their front teeth had been. But soon they began to climb, laughing, all over their father. He sat back in his easy chair and let them romp all over his lap. They hung from his arms, climbed around his neck, their little flowered dresses riding up, exposing the perfect young limbs, the tiny underpants with pictures of Disney characters on them.

The Captain laughed too, and covered his little girls with kisses. He took first one and then the other into his arms, fixed his mouth to their neck, and blew hard, making a loud, obscene noise that delighted them. They squealed and cackled and begged for more. Victor stared in amazement at their beautiful skin, their innocent, open faces. Their cries were miniature parodies of the Sanchez woman's shrieks.

Why had his uncle brought him here? Officers were not supposed to fraternize with enlisted men. Perhaps he intended it as a carrot to dangle in front of him. The lace curtains, the polished wood, the flowered chintz— you too can have all this, if you lead a respectable life in the army. A loving wife and pretty children, these too could be yours in return for loyal service.

His aunt called them to dinner. They sat around an antique oak table, and the Captain made the sign of the cross and bowed his head. The little girls copied him and bowed their heads, showing the perfectly symmetrical parts in their shining hair. "Oh Lord, for this food and for all thy mercies, may we be truly thankful."

All thy mercies. Just that morning, the Sanchez woman had screamed through a long session with the General. Over and over, she had begged them to stop. Over and over, Victor was ordered to turn the dial.

"Mother of God," she had said during the questioning. "You were raised Catholic, were you not? Where is your Christian charity?"

Tito had jeered. The others had laughed nervously.

"The Mother of God does not care about terrorists."

"Is that what the priests taught you in school? That God loves only soldiers?"

"He doesn't give a shit about whores like you," Tito said, and spit on her.

"What about Mary Magdalene? And the woman he saved from stoning? But no, you are all free of sin, aren't you. What would Our Lord say to you about inflicting pain like this?"

Victor saw a worried look creep into Lopez's face.

She kept on at them, her voice ragged and raw from all the screams. "Did you not do the stations of the cross when you were children? Did you not think about the sufferings of Our Lord? Or are you on the side of those who tormented him?"

"Maybe that's enough for today," Lopez muttered.

"You going to listen to this whore?" the Captain had yelled at him. "You want to show her mercy? Fine. We'll stop the machine for today." He snapped his fingers at Yunques. "Go fetch our little friend. On the double." He leaned over the woman. "You want mercy? I'll show you the kind of mercy we reserve for terrorists. Today, you get to go to the zoo."

Yunques came back with a rat in a small cage. The woman's legs were forced apart, and at an order from the Captain, Lopez shoved the animal into her.

"How do you like that?" Captain Peña had shouted over her screams. "You happy now? Any more religious instruction you want to impart?"

And now the same man bent his balding head over his dinner, giving thanks to the Lord. Now, surrounded by the comfortable smells of grilled steak and onions, the sound of classical music streaming from hidden speakers, the piping voices of his little girls, Victor imagined himself saying to Mrs. Peña, "You know your husband is a rapist? A torturer?"

He would not be believed, of course. The Captain, pouring milk for his daughters with the same hand that fixed electrodes to the Sanchez woman's nipples, seemed aware of no contradictions. He fixed his twins' barrettes with the same hand that had twisted the dial.

"I'm so glad you could come, Victor," his aunt said to him with her heartbreaking smile. "In wartime, it's even more important to stay in touch with relatives, don't you think?"

"Oh, yes," Victor said, and smiled in return. "And such wonderful food."

The Captain had reached out and touched his wife's arm without looking at her. A gesture of complete confidence and affection.

This is why he has brought me here, Victor said to himself. This is what he wants me to see. My uncle wants to reassure me that it is possible to perform the work of the little school and yet be a good husband, a kind father, a delightful host in a house filled with love.

EIGHT

AFTER LUNCH THE FOLLOWING DAY, Victor led the
Sanchez woman to the interrogation room. She no longer
put up any struggle, trailing meekly along behind him. He
wondered if this was the first sign of defeat. Then again,
perhaps it was just a tactic, perhaps she was simply con-
serving her energy, the better to withstand the General.

Victor sat her down on the chair. When he turned
around, he was surprised to see a white-haired gentleman in a white jacket standing beside the table where
his uncle was seated.

His uncle nodded at the gentleman, and he lifted a
black bag from the floor. It was the doctor. Victor had
not recognized him, because the last time he had seen
him, the doctor's hair had been black, slicked back.
Now it was quite white, and he had shaved off his moustache. Perhaps these changes of appearance were to
convince himself that he was a different man each time,

that he had no history of working at the little school.

The woman took off her clothes when ordered. The doctor opened his leather bag and wrapped a blood-pressure cuff around her small bicep.

"You are a doctor?" she said in disbelief as she felt the cuff. "What can a doctor be doing in this place?"

"Relax, please. I am just here to examine you." He pumped up the cuff and looked at the meter. "Your blood pressure is slightly high. Nothing to worry about."

"Doctor, I request that you do a thorough examination. You will find that I have been repeatedly raped."

"Just relax, please." He adjusted her slightly forward and placed his stethoscope on her back. "Take a deep breath?" He moved the stethoscope slightly. "And another? That's it. Very good."

She obeyed him like a child, lifting her chin slightly when he placed the metal disc on her chest. His eyes focused somewhere beyond the wall of the interrogation room, as if her heartbeat were a radio signal from a distant town.

"Did you hear what I said, Doctor? I said I've been raped by these men. Over and over again they have raped me. And they put things inside me."

"We'll shove a pitchfork in your guts if you don't shut up." Tito smacked her hard across the back of the head.

"Please," the doctor said. "I am trying to examine this woman."

"I have been deprived of sleep. I have been deprived of water. I have been fed poisoned food."

The doctor took her wrist and held it lightly to take her pulse. He stared at his watch and the woman fell into a silence. Despite the blindfold, Victor could see that she was weeping, undone by the touch of a hand that was not brutal.

The doctor stood up and nodded at Captain Peña. He dropped his stethoscope into his leather bag, snapped it shut, and started for the door. The Captain touched his arm. "Not just yet, Doctor. I want to know how she holds up to the General."

"I don't like to do that. I told you, it is against my oath."

"Sit down, please."

The doctor sat down beside the Captain and stared at the floor.

"Soldier." The Captain pointed at Victor. "You work the dial." When Victor hesitated, his uncle screamed at him. "Do as I say. Do it now."

Victor sat down before the little black box while Tito attached the electrodes, one to a nipple, one between her legs. "Little bitch," he said. "Now you will feel something worth talking about."

"Why?" she asked in a small voice. "Why do you want to hurt me so much?"

"Because you're a terrorist slut and we hate your guts, that's why."

The Captain nodded at Victor. Victor stared at the white numerals. He turned the dial to one and a half.

"Turn it up," his uncle yelled over her screams.

Victor turned it to two, then switched it off.

"I didn't say to stop, you fool. Put it back on."

The woman's screams sank like pencils into Victor's ears.

Afterwards, she sagged in the chair.

Once more the doctor took out his stethoscope and listened to her heart, felt her pulse. The white hair gave him a kindly look—like a doctor in an ad for children's cough syrup. "Her heart is strong," he informed the Captain. "You may continue."

"A little higher this time, soldier."

Victor turned the dial to two and a half and kept it there for a minute. His guts turned to liquid at the sounds she made. Like your flesh is splitting open, the Captain had said. This woman has done nothing to me, and I am splitting her flesh wide open.

The ritual of the stethoscope was repeated. The signal to begin was repeated.

Victor kept his eyes on the white arc of numerals, the pointed dial. He remembered where he had seen such an instrument before. It was in a shop window—the transformer of a toy train set that circled over and over again around the window.

The doctor took the woman's pulse once more before he snapped his black bag shut for the last time and left. Captain Peña went with him, leaving Tito in charge.

"Fucking asshole doctor," Lopez said. "Changing his appearance every time he comes. What's he think they invented blindfolds for?"

"Stop yapping," Tito said. "We got a new toy today." He pulled a pair of handcuffs from his pocket and dangled them in the light like a necklace. These were not the simple loops of thong they were used to; these were shiny steel handcuffs.

Lopez whistled. He took the cuffs from Tito and looked them over. "Smith & Wesson. Nothing but the best for little Miss Sanchez."

"We'll hang the bitch up there." Tito pointed to a heating pipe that ran along the ceiling near the blacked-out windows. They had to stand her on a table, which was not easy since she could barely stand at all. They unclasped one of the handcuffs and slipped it over the pipe, then closed the cuff once more around her wrist. Then they took the table away and she was hanging from both wrists.

"Now let me show you how an expert does it," Tito said. He shoved Victor aside and sat self-importantly at the controls, as if he were about to pilot a jet. "Write down everything she says. Everything I say and everything she says."

Victor opened the pad and took a pencil from the jar. It needed sharpening, but he didn't sharpen it because he remembered what Labredo had suffered at the point of a pencil. Yunques attached the electrodes to her feet.

Tito had apparently decided the way to get an answer out of the woman was not with long shocks but with lots of short, hard bursts. Every time he turned the dial, her feet jerked in a froglike spasm, causing her to swing from the overhead pipe.

Between the sounds of her screams and the shouted questions, Victor's pencil rasped on the paper. What he took down was repetitive.

What is your name?

No. Please.

Tell us your name.

No. Please. I beg you.

Tell us your name.

Please, stop. I beg you, I beg you, I beg you.

What is your name?

Victor took it upon himself to remove Tito's expletives from the questions. And nothing he wrote conveyed the woman's screams, her choking, her tears. The agony of Miss Sanchez would not be part of the official record, he realized, because he did not know how to spell the sound of a scream.

What is your name?

Mother of God. Mother of God. I can't take any more.

Tell us your name.

Dear God, help me. Help me.

Tell us your name.

Maria Sanchez. Stop, please. Have mercy. I beg you.

Tell us your real name.

I am nothing. Nobody. I have no name. Dear God, dear God, dear God.

And so the transcript continued, for ten pages.

After each jolt, between each question and each answer, she swung back and forth from the pipe like a side of beef. The jolts Tito administered were so short that there was no hope of her losing consciousness, but each shock kicked the breath out of her. Eventually a vein opened in her wrist. Blood ran in dark scarlet ribbons down her left arm, formed red squiggles over her rib cage and down her legs, until it fell in big constant drops from her left foot.

The woman was probably not even aware that she was bleeding, but Victor could see that the gore frightened Tito—he had no orders to kill her, or even to mark her.

The sergeant ordered her taken down, and she collapsed in the blood at her feet. He kicked her, not hard. "You piece of shit. You've messed up my nice clean floor. I want you to clean it up, or I'll string you up again."

She could neither talk nor move. She was adjusted so that she was leaning against the wall, and water was brought for her to drink. A cold cloth was placed on her forehead.

"Clean that floor, you bitch. We're making you our cleaning lady, got it? Take the cuffs off before she totally destroys them."

The cuffs, no longer shiny, were undone.

Tito grabbed her hand and slapped it into the crimson puddle. "You feel that? That's your mess, and you're going to clean it up right now."

"Give me a rag," she moaned. "Something to wipe it up."

"A rag? Who said anything about a rag? You don't get no rag." The sergeant's boot was on the back of her neck. He pushed her forward, forcing her face down to the floor in the Muslim attitude of prayer. Her face was an inch from the blood. "You don't get no rag, bitch. You got to use your imagination."

Under the humming fluorescent lights, as the small pointed tongue lapped at the floor, the woman's face was reflected in the dark red blood, the blindfold a black rectangle across her eyes, like a censor's mark.

NINE

THAT DAY WAS A DAY of visitors. First the doctor and then, after they had forced the Sanchez woman to lick up her blood, Victor was summoned to the Captain's office to meet with an American who was introduced as Mr. Wheat.

Mr. Wheat, Victor thought, must be of Irish descent. He reminded him of a Jesuit who had taught him history in the ninth grade. He had the same straw-coloured hair that flopped boyishly over one eyebrow. He had the same serviceable-looking glasses, nothing fashionable about them. He looked like a man who read a lot, a man who liked books.

Despite this intellectual appearance, Mr. Wheat carried with him an invisible cloud of toothpaste and aftershave. He had a ready smile, flawless teeth and a strong hand with which he squeezed Victor's in greeting. Victor wished he could impress this man somehow, and knew sadly that he could not.

"Mr. Wheat is with the American embassy."

"I'm very honoured to meet you, sir."

"Glad to know you, soldier. The Captain tells me you have someone I ought to meet."

"The so-called Sanchez woman," the Captain said. "Bring her in so Mr. Wheat can speak to her himself. Clean her up first."

Victor got Yunques to help him drag the woman up the hall past the Captain's closed door. He wondered what would happen to that flawless smile if Mr. Wheat could have seen them. The woman's heels left bloody streaks along the floor.

She couldn't stand, so they filled the tub in the soldiers' bathroom. He and Yunques lowered her into the water, and she fell back against the tiles.

"Wake up," Yunques snapped. "Wash yourself." But the woman only moaned in response. He turned to Victor. "You deal with her. I'm going for a smoke."

Pink streaks threaded into the water from the woman's body. Victor soaped up a cloth and put it in her hand, but she only let the hand fall into the water. He lifted her left foot from the water and began to wash it. There was a burn mark on her big toe where the electrode had been attached, and he found another burn when he rinsed the blood from her chest.

Gradually, the woman began to revive and was able to wash herself. Her skin glistened under the water, and Victor felt a sexual stirring. He turned away.

He sat on the toilet while she rubbed the bar of soap

all over her hair and rinsed it off, leaning back gingerly so as not to soak her blindfold. He allowed himself a glance at her breasts, the prominent ribs. Such a vulnerable thing, the human body—particularly a woman's; it was a great wrong to torment it. She was not so different from himself, this woman; she was not a campesino. He imagined her as a child, growing up in a small middle-class home like his own. Perhaps she was teased by an older brother, annoyed by a younger sister. Parents had loved her, looked after her, comforted her when she was sick. Not so different from himself. Clearly, she was educated. He imagined her carrying books, arguing with the nuns at school.

And look at the school she was in now, with the likes of Tito and himself for her teachers. And lessons no human being should have to learn.

Victor handed the woman a towel, and when she had dried herself, he bandaged her wrist and gave her back her clothes.

He and Yunques brought her down the hall to the Captain's office. Mr. Wheat was seated near the window, so that the sunlight flashed on his blond hair and made his teeth gleam. He looked utterly out of place in the little school, and Victor found himself staring at him almost as if he were a beautiful woman.

"Where did you pick her up?" Wheat asked the Captain.

"Near the cathedral. She was carrying food supplies."

"Food for children," she said in her cracked, ugly voice. "Apparently this counts as a crime in our country."

"Shut up," the Captain said quietly. "Nobody's talking to you."

"She's connected with the rebels?" Wheat asked.

"Most definitely. We are just waiting for her to admit it."

"And her name is Sanchez."

"So she claims. We don't yet know her real name. We just brought her in last night."

"That is a lie," the woman said. "I have been here at least five days. They are torturing me." She held up the bandaged wrist.

"Resisting arrest," the Captain said. "She put up quite a struggle. It took three men to subdue her."

Victor was surprised by the lie. The Captain too seemed to feel the need to impress this shining American.

"I did not resist arrest," the woman said. "I was distributing food for children. Everything else this man says is a lie."

Less than half an hour ago she had been screaming in agony; she must know such boldness could only bring more of the same. Sometimes bravery seemed to Victor a species of stupidity—but of course it would be convenient for a coward to view it that way.

Mr. Wheat flicked his hair, wafting a little lime-scented aftershave in Victor's direction. "Miss Sanchez, if that's your name—I represent the United States of America. Believe me, we're doing everything we can to ease things up down here for you people."

"Really? Maybe you could untie my hands, then."

Wheat raised his eyebrows at Captain Peña, who shook his head.

"The fact is," Wheat continued, "I only want to know one thing from you."

"I can't tell you anything. I don't know anything."

"Be quiet and listen. For some time now it has been apparent to us that the FMLN leadership has advance knowledge of embassy statements and embassy functions. They know who is visiting, where and for how long—sometimes within twenty-four hours of our own knowledge."

"What you expect me to do about this, I can't imagine."

"I want to know the source of this leak."

"Why ask me, if you believe nothing I say? You really think I was resisting arrest? There's a little room down the hall. If you go there now, you will see my blood all over the floor."

"I'm not interested in any little room. If you simply answer questions truthfully, things will go better for you."

"I was taking food to the cathedral. Food for children orphaned by war. Why don't you talk to them? I'm sure they'd like to thank you in person for everything you've done."

"Listen. Who do you think pays the bills around here? With all due respect to the Captain, we pay the bills around here, and what we say goes. The sooner you understand that, the sooner you'll be out of here. But you have to co-operate."

"I'll co-operate. I'll tell you everything I know."

"You say you were bringing food to the church for orphans of the war?"

"Yes."

"Who asked you to help out?"

"No one. There are signs all over the church asking for volunteers."

"What specifically made you want to help out?"

"The fact that they are orphans. Is the United States against feeding children?"

"I'll ask the questions. Who invited you to be part of this humanitarian effort?"

"I told you. No one. I volunteered. All I do is collect a few cans of food and bring them to the church basement."

Wheat looked at the Captain, shaking his head at her obstinacy. Then he turned back to the woman. "Who asked you to volunteer?"

"No one. Why is that so hard to believe? If I make up a name to please you, they will just beat me when they find out it is false. If I give you the name of a real person who has nothing to do with me or the orphans or the rebels, that person will be arrested and tortured just like me. But you still won't have whatever it is you want."

"I want to know the source of the embassy leak."

"I wish I could help you."

"Do you know a woman named Teresita Sanchez?"

"Teresita Sanchez. No."

"Teresita Sanchez-Vega."

"I don't know her."

"Are you sure you want to stick with that story?"

"It's not a story. It's just the way it is."

"She's a typist at the embassy."

"I'm glad. Jobs are precious these days."

"I'm asking you if you know her."

"And I'm telling you the truth. I do not know her."

"Your name is Sanchez, her name is Sanchez. And you don't know her?"

"It's a common name. Surely you know this."

"San Salvador is not that big a town."

"It's two million people!"

"You have the same last name."

"I don't know her. If I did, I would not deny it, because I have no dealings with this person, no connection whatsoever. I wish I could tell you yes, if that would get me out of here."

"You said you would co-operate."

"Believe me, I'm trying to. At this moment I want nothing more than to please you, to make you feel that I am trying to help you by telling the truth."

"This is what you call co-operation?"

"Please. Just entertain for a moment the possibility that I am not lying. Ask yourself what I have to gain and what I have to lose."

"You know exactly what you have to gain. So tell me the truth: do you know Teresita Sanchez-Vega?"

"No, sir. I don't."

"This is not co-operation. I'm going to let you think about it some more. I'll ask you again in ten days."

"I don't think so. By then I will be dead."

"Get her out of my sight," Wheat said.

The Captain snapped his fingers, and Yunques led her away to the cells.

"She has a real attitude problem," Wheat said when she was gone. "Real hard case, that one."

"To tell you the truth," the Captain said, "we don't suspect this prisoner of any connection to the embassy. We only suspect her of taking food to the enemy."

"But we had this Sanchez at the embassy. We were sure she was the leak."

"And now you're not sure?"

"Little Miss Sanchez was killed, see. But the leaks started up again."

"You killed her?"

"I resent that, Captain. What kind of outfit do you think we run?"

"Forgive me. You thought she was a spy, she was killed, naturally I thought . . ."

"She was raped and murdered on her way home one night. Terrible thing."

"Terrible."

"Of course, the fact that the leaks started up again after she died doesn't necessarily put her in the clear."

"No. There could be more than one leak."

"I want you to hang on to this Sanchez prisoner. You understand, I'm under a lot of pressure to plug that leak."

"I understand."

"And if I can ever do anything for you one day, well, one hand washes the other, right, Captain?"

"Right. We will keep on her, Mr. Wheat. Don't you worry."

TEN

THE AMERICAN'S VISIT was so brief as to seem hallucinatory. One moment he was there, the next he was nothing but a memory of blond hair and a whiff of aftershave. When he was gone, the soldiers had their lunch, and then in the afternoon the woman was brought back to the interrogation room, where they left her alone, tied to the chair. Tito liked to make her wait like this, knowing the torture would come but not knowing when or what form it would take. After half an hour, maybe forty-five minutes, they connected her up to the machine as if she were herself an electronic device without which the little school could not run.

Once again Victor took down a record of the interrogation while Tito worked the dial. All through the woman's screams and the shouted questions, Victor felt a growing thickness in the back of his throat like an oncoming cold. And at the crown of his head there was a sore spot as if he had been tapped with a small, hard object there. Much of what he wrote was blurred with sweat.

Then Tito shocked the woman too hard and she fainted. When they could not revive her, Lopez and Victor carried her to her cell.

"Too bad the whore is not on our side," Lopez muttered. "She is one tough bitch."

Victor was glad to be on guard duty while his colleagues interrogated other prisoners. He could hear the mutter of gunfire from the nearby rifle range, and the odd sergeant's shout from the garrison. He sat at the little table, his head in his hands, feeling himself sink into a fever as if toward the bottom of the sea. He hardly noticed when they came for Ignacio Perez, the man in the cell across from the woman's. Perez was the only prisoner there who seemed to Victor as if he might actually be a guerrilla. He was not much older than Victor, short but powerfully built, and he resisted the soldiers like a wild dog, kicking and screaming at them.

Victor's brow was hot as an iron in his hand. He barely heard the shouts and cries coming from what used to be the little school's playground. They were playing Submarine with Perez. So far, Victor had not had to participate in that particular game, where one or two soldiers would toss the prisoner into the tank of water that had been fouled with every kind of filth the school could produce. The prisoner was then forced beneath the surface at the end of a restraining pole, and held there until he near drowned in the shit and piss. Who thought these games up, Victor had wondered when it had first been explained to him. But this day he hardly noticed Tito's laughter or Perez's terrified, choked cries.

Later, when Lopez came to relieve him, he sat down at the table with a weary sigh. He looked Victor up and down. "What's wrong with you, Peña?"

"Nothing. Except I just . . ." Victor had to lean on the back of the chair to steady himself. His words were slurring like those of a drunk. "I think maybe I'm getting a cold or something."

"You're shivering like a—"

Victor didn't hear what Lopez said next, because a gauzy curtain closed between them. He felt a smile spreading like butter across his face, and then his legs folded beneath him.

For the next three days he lay in bed, clenched in a fever, except for the times when he dragged himself to the barracks toilet. At his lowest point he perched on the toilet while at the same time leaning over a bucket, discharging violently from both ends.

In bed, dreams and memories intermingled. He dreamed of his uncle's appearing to him like an angel of deliverance at the military prison. He dreamed of Mr. Wheat walking among the bodies of El Playón amid a scent not of death but of aftershave. Spirits rose like steam from the bodies, calling Victor to join them—death wasn't so bad, it wasn't so bad once you got used to it. It was better than being afraid all the time. In the distance, a woman called a name he couldn't quite make out.

The doctor visited him. Later, Victor wasn't sure if it had been real, because the doctor had grown a small moustache and his hair was black again. But it must have been real, because there was a bottle of medicine on a small wooden box that was his bedside table. It tasted like licorice and made the dreams even more vivid.

That night he climbed out of bed, the fever gone, and tiptoed through completely deserted classrooms that glowed pale as marble in the moonlight. After slitting the throat of the night guard, a boy of fifteen, he opened the last door and lay in bed with the Sanchez woman. What they did together was indistinct, but he had a wonderful sensation of warmth and comfort, as if he were curled in a den of warm animals.

When the Captain and the others burst in on them, Victor pulled out his service revolver and fired before they could even draw their pistols. Bodies tumbled at his feet. He pulled the Sanchez woman along the corridor, fighting hand to hand with the soldiers who now leapt out at him from all sides. It was amazing what strength and cunning he had. Bullets swarmed in the air, but he ran through them with supernatural courage. It should have been a terrifying dream, but it was not; the sense of victory was too thrilling.

But the thrill dissolved when he awoke and remembered he was a coward. A coward who, far from saving the Sanchez woman, had done his part to split open her flesh.

He lay in bed trying to persuade himself that he was not evil. He was not doing it by choice. He was here under threat of death. If he tried to help her escape, they would both be shot; that was not good. If he tried to escape himself, he would be shot, and *that* was not good. Besides, if he disappeared, they would only replace him with someone much worse. Nevertheless, he resolved to escape if the chance—a realistic chance—should ever present itself.

Victor suffered three days of fever before he was pronounced fit to return to duty. He went back to work feeling thin and ethereal, no match for the harshness of his fellow soldiers.

"Hey, Peña junior," said Yunques. "How was your vacation?"

"Not much fun, thanks."

"You're lucky the Captain's your uncle, Peña." Tito made a throat-slitting gesture. "Me and the boys here get the feeling you're a slacker. A malingerer."

"That isn't true. I was sick. Lopez, you saw."

Lopez shrugged and looked out the window. "So you fainted. So you have a weak stomach."

"Tell me, Peña," said Tito. "What do you have in mind for a career after you leave the army?"

"I don't know. I haven't thought about it much."

"Because, to tell you the truth, I get a very negative feeling from you. You don't participate here like you should."

"And if you don't participate in one way," Yunques put in, "you will certainly participate in another."

"Peña and the doctor, I think they are two of a kind. I think we should tie them together and throw them in the tank." Tito kicked his chair. "Funny how you manage to be out sick just when things get interesting."

"What do you mean?"

"It reminds me of your battle experience, no? You manage to be unconscious just when things take a turn for the worse? Oh, yes, don't look so shocked. I happen to have a friend in the Casarossa unit. He's told me all about you, my friend, and frankly, you are going to have to convince me of your sincerity. If you're just here because your uncle saved your ass, that makes you a security threat."

"I don't understand. What are you talking about?"

"Look. We're not fools here, just because we don't read faggot books in English. We know that when this war is over, people will come asking questions about special units like ours. What are you going to tell them, eh? 'I was helpless'? 'They made me do it'? 'I never hurt anybody'?"

"I won't tell anybody anything. I assume everything we do here is strictly confidential."

"What we do here is not confidential. It doesn't even exist. As far as I'm concerned, you are not yet part of this team. You never do anything to anybody."

"That's not true. I worked the General on Sanchez."

"The Captain made you do it. First opportunity you get, you're going to blab to everybody what went on here."

"That's not true either. I'm on your side. I wouldn't be here otherwise."

"Oh, yeah? We'll see about that."

He and Lopez had guardroom duty that afternoon. Lopez was always more friendly to him when the others weren't around.

"What did Tito mean about my leaving just when things got interesting? Did she talk, the Sanchez woman?"

"No, she didn't. She seems determined to die, this bitch. It's unaccountable." Lopez could come out with words like that once in a while. Talk like a complete thug and then suddenly he would use a word that sounded like the tattered remains of an education.

"She had more meetings with the General?"

"Not just the General. She's made the Captain angry now. It's becoming personal now, and that's much worse for her. We did the water thing to her—have you seen that yet?"

"No."

"Put a wet towel over her face, pour water all over it. Basically drowns them without killing them. She choked and cried like a motherfucker but didn't tell us a thing."

"Maybe she really knows nothing. Maybe she is innocent."

"Don't be an idiot. If she was innocent, she would have told us everything she knows. She would have given up her grade three teacher by now, if she was innocent." Lopez laughed at some memory. "When the rat trick doesn't work, you *know* they've got to be FMLN. Let me tell you, I wish I had as much balls as this bitch."

"Maybe she will never talk. Maybe some people—"

"Don't be stupid. You think she's going to continue this way if we take her eye out with a pencil? We're just going easy on her because she's a woman. We can afford to take time. Otherwise they turn you into a monster, and that's no good. Then it's like the bastards have won—the rebels, I mean. If they turn you into a monster, it's like all the things they've been saying about us are true. But listen, my friend." Lopez leaned forward and spoke in a quieter voice. "If I were you, I'd worry more about myself. Tito is going to have your nuts in a vise if you don't participate more. I mean it. He don't like what he's heard about you. He don't trust you. This afternoon you better show some enthusiasm or, you know, there might be an accident one night—a grenade or something."

They listened for the rest of the morning to the sounds from the interrogation room. There was a tea party with cookies for one of the male prisoners. A tea party was a regular beating; a tea party with cookies was a beating with clubs.

When they dragged him back to the cells, Victor could not see a single mark on his face.

ELEVEN

WHEN THE WOMAN was first brought to the little school, she had been wearing a watch that hung loosely on her left wrist until the Captain had taken it from her. He brought it to the interrogation room, pulling it out of a manila envelope. It was a large man's watch, a Bulova with gold trim and a gold flexible band. It was engraved on the back: *To M. from J.*

The Captain read the inscription aloud. "Who is this J.?" he asked her. "Who is this J. who gave you the watch?"

"José. José was my brother. He is dead now."

"Brothers do not give watches to their sisters," the Captain said. "Nor do they engrave them."

He asked her the question over and over, and every time she gave the same answer.

Captain Peña said to Victor, "Clearly, the M. is just to convince us her name is really Maria, although we know it is not Maria. The J., however, is another matter. This J. could be a real person, and I want to know who it is."

"I told you. It is my brother, José."

"Listen," the Captain said to her. "Maybe you can win your smelly little watch back." He unbound her thumbs and slid the watch over her left wrist. "All you have to do is tell us what we want to know."

"You wanted his name," she said. "I gave you his name."

Captain Peña kicked her in the shin—it would have looked childish had it not been done with such force. For the next few minutes the woman sucked in her breath through clenched teeth.

Victor had not seen her for the three days he was sick, and he was shocked by the change in her appearance. Her face had taken on a grey, corpse-like hue, and the set of her features had changed utterly. Where before they had had a fixed, determined look, now they were slack and puffy. The woman's words were still defiant, but the sag of her shoulders and the slack muscles of her cheeks resembled only death. It was as if the spirit had already left her body, and what defiance remained was only reflex.

Perhaps courage itself is just a reflex, Victor thought, and cowardice too. No credit or blame could attach where there was only reflex. Neither the brave nor the cowardly would be responsible for their actions. She was not a saint, and he was not a demon.

"Hit her," Captain Peña said to Victor.

Victor was caught off guard. He had sat himself down

at the table with pencil in hand, ready as always to play secretary. "Pardon me, Captain?"

"You heard me. Hit her."

The other soldiers folded their arms across their chests and watched.

Victor put down his pencil and walked around the table. An actual physical blow—his fist against her flesh—would be harder to administer than a shock. More personal. The woman tensed at his approaching footsteps.

Victor punched her in the belly, not too high. She doubled over.

"I said hit her, not tickle her. She didn't even feel it." Captain Peña stepped back against the wall, folded his arms like the others, and stared at Victor.

Tito moved away from the woman and stood beside the Captain. Then Yunques and Lopez moved to the opposite wall. He felt their eyes sink into him like fangs.

Victor's terror expressed itself in a fury of punches. The woman had no time to recover from one before another caught her somewhere else. Some part of Victor still kept the blows low—the ribs, the side, the hip. He meant to give her a good one in the chest—a convincing punch that would knock her back against the wall without doing too much damage—but the woman chose that moment to tip forward and his punch connected with her face. He felt her tooth break the skin on his knuckles and he also felt the tooth snap. The woman tumbled back against the wall, cracking her head against it, blood pouring from her upper lip.

Cheers and whistles filled the room.

Victor staggered a little in the centre of the room, thrown off balance by his own violence.

Captain Peña bent over the groaning woman and pulled the watch from her wrist. He handed it to Victor with great solemnity, as if it were a medal of honour. "Good work, soldier. Such work calls for a little bonus."

Lopez and Yunques gave him a thumbs-up sign, and even Tito gave his shoulder a squeeze. What gorgeous relief, their sudden acceptance of him—like cool water on a burn.

That night, the watch ticked loudly on the wooden crate beside Victor's bed. It took him a long time to fall asleep, and the night was filled with bad dreams. In one, Tito was playing Submarine with him, half drowning him in the filthy tank. He awoke with a shout, and lay staring into the blackness until his heart subsided. Outside it was raining, the drops rattling on the garbage cans outside his window. The breeze brought smells not of the tank but of the nearby pastures.

The dial of the woman's watch glowed in the dark: four-thirty. Would she be asleep now? Or was she kept awake by the pain of the beating he had given her? Punching a defenceless woman in the mouth, you couldn't get much lower than that. He squeezed the watch tightly, and felt it ticking in his fist like a tiny heart.

When they drove into town the next morning, Victor was so tired he could hardly keep his eyes open. Sunlight poured through the Cherokee's windows, and even through the tinted glass it felt hot. The heat made Victor even sleepier. This was the first time the squad had driven anywhere since El Playón. They did not usually venture out in daylight, but today was special. They were all dressed in impeccable uniforms, and in the back of the Cherokee they had two bewildered male prisoners, freshly scrubbed and wearing new clothing.

It was a big day. So big that Captain Peña had held a full-dress inspection first thing in the morning. He had yelled at them about the state of their uniforms, yelled at them to shine their boots until they were mirrors, were they a bunch of animals? Now the cleaned and pressed squad was heading into town and, despite his drowsiness, Victor could feel the pride inside the Cherokee. He indulged a fantasy, imagining himself part of a crack unit rolling into town for a victory celebration.

One of the cleaned-up prisoners was Ignacio Perez, whom Tito had nearly drowned playing Submarine. Victor had seen his papers. The other man was much older and had only one arm. Victor recognized him from the group cell that held half a dozen prisoners, but he knew nothing about him. Neither of the men was blindfolded, and they crouched in the back with heads averted from the light.

The square in front of the Presidential Palace was already crowded. Coloured strips of bunting were woven around the iron gates, and off to one side a brass band was playing. Sunlight flashed on their instruments.

Tito showed the guards his pass and they were allowed through. A stage had been set up in front of the palace. Tito drove around behind it and parked.

"All right, you faggots," he said to the prisoners. "Make sure you smile a lot, you got that?"

The prisoners nodded.

"You got to smile like you love us, understand?" Tito grabbed Perez by the hair. "Understand?"

"Yes, I understand," Perez said.

"You'd better. Otherwise, we're going to pay a visit to your daughters later—show up at the plantation and cut their tits off. How you like that, huh?"

"Please, sergeant. We will smile the whole time."

"You make it convincing, though."

"Otherwise we cut up your daughters," Yunques said, as if he had just thought of it.

Tito gave Perez several light slaps on the cheek, as if reviving him from a faint. "It should be easy for you to smile! No more Submarine! No more tea party! You should be happy! Today you get to go free—unlike your buddies back at the school."

A row of seats had been reserved for the squad just behind the front row. They filed in and sat down. Captain Peña turned around and looked them over from the front row. He didn't smile, just nodded at Tito and turned around again to face the stage.

The stage was not large. Most of the space was taken up by flags: the flag of El Salvador, the flag of the United Nations, the flag of the United States. Several dignitaries sat down in the handful of seats. Victor caught a glimpse of blond hair flashing in the sunlight and recognized Mr. Wheat, the American who had visited the little school.

Members of the foreign media, as glamorous to Victor as movie stars, were there in abundance. Photographers crouched before the stage taking preliminary readings. The air was alive with expectation. The band played another march, and Victor rubbed at his knuckles where the woman's teeth had cut him.

Then the President of El Salvador came out onstage and took a seat. He waved in acknowledgement of the applause, but he did not address the audience. One of his ministers—a balding man in an impeccable pin-stripe suit—stood before the microphone. Victor didn't know his name, but he had seen his photograph many times.

The minister spoke first on the dignity of labour. He noted how the nation could not survive without the people who worked the soil. It was in recognition of this fact that the present administration was committed to land reform. The President nodded his head in agreement; Mr. Wheat stared impassively at the crowd.

"Today's ceremony," the minister went on, "is not a great moment in history. We are not gathered at a great turning point. What we celebrate today is simply a quiet example of quiet justice: under our Land to the Tiller program, those who work the land . . ." Here he paused for effect. " . . . will own the land."

Tito and Lopez escorted the two prisoners to the side of the stage. The one-armed prisoner was sent up first, his features fixed in a grotesque jack-o'-lantern smile.

The minister held up a scroll and spoke not to the prisoner but to the audience. "Señor Bartel, this deed transfers ownership of one-tenth of the land you have worked for the past twenty years to you and your family. On this piece of land you may plant what you want. Or, if you choose, you may sell this land for whatever the market will pay. Any profit from this piece of land goes directly into your pocket."

Turning to the prisoner for the first time, the minister handed him his deed. The prisoner kept smiling and nodding his head. The document joined their two hands, and a lusty round of applause went up. Camera flashes lit the backdrop.

The one-armed prisoner took his seat again, and then a man Victor recognized as General Damont stepped up to the microphone. Damont was in charge of El Salvador's anti-terrorist strategy. He had a grave, courteous manner. He thanked the minister and the President for teaching him the wisdom of reform. "Justice and wisdom," the General said, "will win this war for me." He was completely unfazed by the stage, the crowd, the cameras, pausing between sentences with the confidence of a seasoned actor. "Justice and wisdom will take from the terrorists the very ground they stand on. How do I know this? The proof of this, my friends, is the constant stream of defectors from the other side."

Ignacio Perez was sent up to the stage.

The General faced him, one warrior to another, and placed the microphone between them. "You were a member of the rebel forces, is that correct?"

"Yes, General. That is true." Perez seemed much more natural than the one-armed man. Nervous, but natural.

"Could someone lower this microphone, please? I want everyone to hear what this man has to say."

A technician was produced. He lowered the microphone to the prisoner's height.

"You were a member of the FMLN, is that correct, Señor Perez?"

"Yes, General, I was a member of the FMLN. But I can no longer fight for these people."

"And why is that? Why can you no longer fight beside them?"

"The last village we were at. The campesinos refused to give them food. So the rebels burned their village to the ground. They killed the old men with bayonets, and they raped all of the girls."

The General nodded gravely. "Tell me this. Why did you join the rebels in the first place?"

"I joined the rebels for one reason. I joined the rebels because they promised us we would have land. Not a lot, but a piece of land of our own to work."

"And now, Señor Perez? Now that your own government has promised you a piece of land?"

"Now I will fight for the government."

"You are volunteering for the army?"

"Yes, General. I regret I ever joined the rebels. They are the enemy of the people and I want to destroy them."

"Well, you are welcome in my battalion any day."

The General held his hands up in ostentatious applause. The dignitaries behind him—even the President—rose and clapped their hands. The entire audience rose to its feet and clapped loud and long. Before the applause could subside, the band struck up the theme from *Rocky*.

The General smiled brilliantly. Seeing this, the prisoner remembered Tito's warning and he smiled brilliantly too. Then, in what looked like a completely spontaneous bit of theatre, the General hugged him. He would not have done so yesterday, Victor thought, when Perez was filthy from Submarine.

The President gave a short speech after that, thanking the Americans for their help and vowing to continue his struggle for reform.

When they were at the Cherokee again, Tito took the deed from the one-armed prisoner. "You'll get it back," he said. "It has to be formally notarized."

Ignacio Perez made to get back into the Cherokee.

"Where you going, you idiot?"

The prisoner looked at him blankly.

"Don't you understand anything? You're free to go."

"Free?"

"Yes, free. Absolutely and completely free. You are a landowner now. We will have the deed notarized and bring it to you tomorrow." He reached out and pumped the prisoner's hand energetically. "So long, Ignacio. No hard feelings, I hope. It's just war, you know, and war . . . war does funny things."

TWELVE

"THANK YOU, MY CHILDREN," Captain Peña said when they were back at the little school. "You were very well behaved, and I'm giving you the afternoon off."

The men made childish noises of approval, slapping each other and mussing each other's hair, although none of them touched Victor.

"That's the good news," the Captain continued. "The bad news is, you have to work tonight." The Captain waited for the exaggerated groans to subside. "Tonight we have another ceremony to attend. A very different ceremony. Tonight we will hand over to Señors Bartel and Perez their deeds of property. Fully notarized. Don't worry, it won't take long."

The sun was still strong outside, so Victor took a book and went to sit at the edge of the pasture under a tree. He read a few paragraphs, but it was such a pretty day, he found himself looking up at the white columns of cloud, the deep blue of the sky above the hills. From a nearby hillock, three heifers gazed at him with melancholy eyes.

So far, it had been a better day than most. True, the land ceremony was something of a sham—all right, it was a complete fake—but at least two prisoners had gone free. And now the Sanchez woman was getting the afternoon off. That was a good thing too. He dozed for a while, and woke when he heard his uncle's footsteps on the gravel road. Victor jumped to his feet and saluted.

"At ease, soldier," the Captain said, and lifted his bottle of chocolate milk as if to say, You see? I know how to relax and take a break. "Beautiful day, isn't it?"

"Yes, sir. A wonderful day, sir."

"If only it were peacetime, I would take the family for a picnic somewhere. The twins love a picnic. They get so excited."

"I can imagine. They are beautiful girls."

Captain Peña gestured with his milk bottle toward Victor's book. "Reading again, I see."

"Yes, sir. It was free time. I never thought—"

"You're right. I did not forbid you from reading on your own time. Still, you disappoint me, Victor."

"I'm sorry, Captain."

"Look, things are very cozy with the Americans right now. You remember Mr. Wheat? Mr. Wheat and I get along very well. We understand each other's needs. There's a chance I may be able to get you into a training course with the Americans."

"In Panama?" Victor's heart began to pound. If he could get to Panama, he might be able to escape altogether. He could escape to the North.

"No, not Panama. The Americans are offering training at Fort Benning. In the United States."

"I heard it was only the Atlacatl battalion going there."

"Maybe yes, maybe no. I am trying to arrange things. Now, do me a favour."

"Yes, sir?"

Captain Peña pulled a packet of matches from his pocket and pressed them into Victor's palm. "Burn that fucking book."

That sad little bonfire spoiled the rest of Victor's afternoon. He lay on his bunk until suppertime, the blackened, curling pages vivid in his mind.

Even as he sat in the driver's seat of the Cherokee, he could still see the title turning brown and then flaring up. He started the truck and waited for the rest of the squad to pile in.

Tito was beside him, clutching the two deeds of property. He had assembled the squad after supper and told them all to change into street clothes but to bring their automatic weapons and side arms. Lopez slid into the back seat, and a moment later Yunques.

"Let's go," Tito said. "I want to get this over with."

"The left headlight isn't working," Victor said.

"Fix it later. Let's go."

The roads were pitch-dark. Driving with one headlight

made Victor nervous. He kept veering to the right, where the one good light wafted over the trees.

In the confined cabin of the truck, the smell of rum was almost overpowering. Tito had spent his free time drinking in town, and now he was in a bad mood at having to cut his festivities short. When Yunques and Lopez started horsing around in the back, he screamed at them to shut up.

They drove to town in a heavy silence. They passed the Presidential Palace, where stray strands of bunting blew from the iron fence.

For the next fifteen minutes the only words uttered in the Cherokee were Tito's barked commands of *left, right here, left.* Each time, he jabbed a thick finger into Victor's line of vision. They were headed in the direction of El Playón, but before they reached the cliffs, they turned up a rutted road at the edge of a plantation.

"Easy, Peña. You'll rip the tailpipe off this thing."

"The road is very bad."

"Easy!"

A mile up the road, they came to a row of shacks, corrugated tin roofs over crumbling adobe walls. The night was as beautiful as the day had been, and men were gathered in groups of three or four around kerosene lanterns in front of the shacks. They stood up at the sound of the approaching truck, their eyes flashing white in the headlights.

"Stop here. As soon as we get out, Peña, you turn this thing around to face the gate. Lopez and Yunques, you cover me. I will deal with these dogs. I want to make this quick."

"You just want to take out the two?"

"We have orders only for the two. Two only, and to pick up the boy."

"What boy is that?" Victor asked. Tito hadn't mentioned any boy in the briefing after supper, but he knew he was often not told things.

"That one there will do." He pointed to a skinny boy in a long white shirt. He had long hair and a pretty mouth that gave him a feminine look. They got out of the Jeep and Victor turned it around.

Tito leaned in the window and breathed rum over everything. "Keep the motor running." He walked over to the gathering of men in front of the shack. The kerosene light cast deep shadows in his eye sockets and turned his face dull yellow. "I need Bartel and Perez. I have their deeds for them."

"Bartel and Perez are not feeling well," one of the men answered. "Perhaps too much celebrating today. I will give them their deeds."

Tito brandished the two scrolls. "These are legal papers. They must be personally delivered. Personally delivered and personally signed for."

"Why do you bring legal papers in the middle of the night? Why are they not in a legal office?"

"You want to make some kind of argument? You want to make trouble?"

"No. We don't want trouble."

"As soon as I give Bartel and Perez these papers, these men are landowners. Landowners, you understand? Haven't you heard of Land to the Tiller?"

"Yes, I have heard of this program. These men own land now?"

"Okay, it's nothing grand. We're not talking about a plantation, here. Just the little acre they've been working. Now, are you going to let me give it to them or you going to make trouble?"

"I am right here." It was Ignacio Perez who spoke from the doorway of the first shack.

"Señor Perez! Good to see you again! I have your deed for you. Come out into the light so everyone can see the new landowner. Soldier," he said to Lopez. "Cuff that boy. The boy comes with us."

"Why do you need the boy? Just give us the papers."

"Where is your buddy Bartel?"

"Señor Bartel is sick. He has a fever. Please. Don't take the boy."

The boy's mother came out and went down on her knees in front of Tito. She began begging and crying.

"Get Bartel out here now. We will give him his deed and then we will go."

"I will give him his deed. I told you, he is sick."

"Use your head, Perez. You want us to search house to house for this guy? People could get hurt. Houses could get destroyed. A fire might break out. Shut up, you whore." He cracked the woman on the skull with his rifle butt, and she lay still at his feet.

Nobody moved.

Victor watched in the rear-view mirror as the one-armed Bartel was brought out, barely able to walk. His face was slick with fever.

"Bartel! Good to see you again! We have your papers for you. Your deed of property."

Tito raised his machine gun and then casually, like a man spraying bugs, flicked his wrist once, twice, and hosed them both down.

Women screamed. Children woke crying. And men ran into the bushes.

"Yunques! Give Señor Perez his deed of ownership."

Yunques knelt in the dirt and opened Perez's mouth, set the scroll in it, and closed the man's jaw on it. He did the same to Bartel. Dead legs twitched.

The road was empty. Just the soldiers and the kerosene lamps.

"Anybody else?" Tito called to the bushes. "Any other faggots out there want a little piece of land? A little piece of property to call home? No?"

Lopez shoved the boy into the back of the truck.

As the others climbed in, there was whimpering from the shacks. From the bushes, nothing but the blowing of the leaves.

THIRTEEN

ON HER TENTH DAY at the little school, the woman broke. By now she was not recognizable as the defiant creature they had dragged into captivity. I have done this to her, Victor thought as he led her into the interrogation room. I have helped in this destruction.

"Today is your lucky day," Captain Peña said when Victor sat her down. Ten days ago she might have responded with bitterness, but now she only hung her head. Dark, matted hair straggled over her face.

"What's the matter, whore?" Tito yanked her head back. "You sleepy? Listen to the Captain!"

"As I say, young lady, today is your lucky day. No one is going to hurt you today. Doesn't that make you happy?"

The woman said nothing. Victor tried to will her to answer. Please reply, he thought. It will go better if you reply.

"I said we're not going to hurt you today. Doesn't that make you happy?" the Captain repeated.

"Answer, whore." Tito pulled on her hair so that her throat was exposed.

"It makes me happy," she said dully. Her voice was now little more than a whisper.

"Louder, please. I can't hear you."

"It makes me happy."

"We are not going to kick you, today. Doesn't that make you happy?"

"It makes me happy."

"We are not going to fuck you. We are not going to pull out your hair. Doesn't that make you happy?"

"It makes me happy."

"We are not going to hang you from the pipes today. Doesn't that make you happy?"

"It makes me happy."

"We are not going to stick any rats inside you, not even any cockroaches. What do you think about that?"

"It makes me very happy."

"And today, the General will not be attaching himself to you. That must make you *very* happy."

"It makes me very happy."

Victor was glad to hear this also, but it was obvious from the Captain's tone that something else was going to happen. Something unpleasant.

"Good," said Captain Peña. "Excellent. Because we want you to be happy. We don't want to hurt you. All we want is for you to tell us your real name. After that, you can fill in the details. Who you report to, who works with you, where you drop off supplies. That kind of thing."

"But I know nothing of these matters. I've told you a thousand times." The woman spoke into her chest, she did not raise her head.

"Yes, a thousand times," the Captain said pleasantly. "A thousand times, and a thousand lies. But today it will all change. It is all about to change, and we are not even going to lay a hand on you. Bring him in."

Now the woman's shoulders jumped a little. And she lifted her face. It was still swollen, the upper lip puffy where Victor had hit her.

Tito opened the door and shouted the Captain's order down the hall. A moment later Yunques brought the boy in, soaking wet. Yunques was not soft like Victor; he would have made sure the boy did not sleep.

"I want you to introduce yourself to this woman."

The boy faced one way then another. It always took the prisoners a while to get used to being blindfolded. They were never sure if they were being spoken to unless they were addressed as *whore* or *faggot*.

"Yes, you. Tell this woman your name."

"My name is Jaime Reyes." The blindfold emphasized the full lips, his girl's mouth.

"Very good," the Captain said. "You're doing very well so far. Now, tell this woman here where you are from."

"I live on the Cuzcatlán plantation. Near El Playón."

"Tell her how old you are."

"I am thirteen years old. I will be fourteen in October."

"Bastard," the woman said quietly.

"Now, now," the Captain said. "There is no need to insult the boy. We have every reason to believe he is a legitimate child of God-fearing parents."

"Do not do this," the woman said. "For your own soul's sake, I beg you, do not do this."

"Thirteen years old, Miss Whoever-you-are. Thirteen years old, this boy. Would you like to turn fourteen?"

"Yes, sir. I will be fourteen in October." The boy was on the edge of tears, and Victor saw that the fabric of his shirt, even though wet, was trembling.

"Thirteen. You must have been confirmed this year."

"Yes, sir. At the cathedral."

"Did the bishop give you a little slap on the cheek?"

"Yes, sir."

"Tell me, I never understood that slap. What does that little slap mean, exactly?"

"It means—it means that our faith will be tested. Our faith will be tested, and we must prepare ourselves."

"Well, I'm glad you are prepared, Mr. Fourteen-in-October. Very glad. As a man of faith, little Jaime, you will be interested to know that this woman here is an incarnation of the Virgin Mary—although I assure you from first-hand experience, she is no longer a virgin. Nevertheless, she has the Blessed Virgin's wonderful power to protect. You know about this? To intercede. Remember this, Jaime. I am God, and this woman here is the Blessed Virgin."

The prisoner strained forward in her chair. "You are evil," she said in her cracked voice. "You are an evil man.

The woman does not live who would knowingly bear you a son."

Captain Peña ignored her. "This woman, little Jaime, this woman can cause you pain, or she can save you from pain. It is *entirely in her power,* I want you to be clear on this. Whether you are in pain or not, whether you shed tears or blood, it is *entirely within her power.*"

"Please don't hurt me, sir. I have done nothing wrong."

"Don't be afraid. I'm sure Our Lady will protect you. Do you have any brothers or sisters, Jaime?"

"Two. Two sisters. They are younger than me."

"No brothers?"

The boy swallowed. Beneath the wet shirt, his breathing was as fast as a rabbit's.

"Answer the Captain, faggot."

"I have one brother, but I don't know where he is. I believe he is with the rebels in Chalatenango."

"A brother with the rebels in Chalatenango. Well, this is an unexpected bonus. What is your brother's name?"

"Dario."

"Dario Reyes. The Blessed Virgin here may be personally acquainted with him. But we don't know, little Jaime, because Our Lady will tell us nothing. That is going to end very soon. Is there anything you would like to say?"

"Please don't hurt me, sir. I am not a rebel. I have done no wrong."

"I believe you. I am sure you are a good boy. That is the whole point. Soldier," he barked at Tito, and the boy's shoulders jerked up to his ears, "what shall we do with him?"

"Hard to say, Captain. There are many possibilities."

"Give me your thoughts. What would be most effective, in your view?"

"How about we cut his thing off. We cut his thing off, we cook it, and then we feed it to the Virgin here. Make her eat it."

"Very imaginative."

"Please don't hurt me, sir. Please—I will do anything you say. Anything you want me to, I'll do." The boy was crying hard, his words wildly distorted.

"Or we could pull his fingernails out. That's very painful."

"It's a little bloodier than I had in mind. And a little slow. I hate to make a mess in here. Look at that, he's pissing his pants."

"You fucking little faggot, I'm going to make you lick that up."

"Leave it for now. Give me some ideas."

"Cocksucker. Pissing on our clean floor. How would you like to meet the General, huh? How about I introduce you to the General right now?"

"Leave him alone," the woman said. "Please. Just let the boy go, and maybe I can tell you some things you want to know."

The Captain, Tito, all the soldiers looked at her. Silence fell over them as they realized that she had offered to talk. The only sounds were the boy's.

"She's talking," Victor said hurriedly. "Let me drag this little faggot back to his cell." He grabbed the boy by his soaking collar.

Captain Peña shrieked, "Leave the boy where he is!" He slapped the woman full force across the face. "You think you make bargains with us? You think maybe you will *negotiate* with us? You whore. I will show you how we negotiate. I will show you exactly how we negotiate. On your back, faggot. Get down on the floor."

The boy was handcuffed, but he began to kick out blindly. His foot connected glancingly with Victor's groin, and he doubled over and groaned, as if the injury were great. Lopez and Tito wrestled the boy to the floor, pinning him down on his back.

"Get his leg up on the bed frame. Just the heel. Get his leg up."

They dragged him across the floor, the boy begging *please, please, please* the whole way. Victor had sunk to his knees with eyes closed. He could hear in the knife-edge of his uncle's voice, in Tito's silence, in the sharp, near-hysterical cries of Lopez and Yunques, that a threshold had been crossed. Violence had been launched. Violence had been launched and was now as impossible to recall as a missile that has been fired.

"Listen to this," Captain Peña yelled in the woman's ear. "You listen close to this sound! If you weren't such a whore, this would not have happened."

The boy's leg was propped up on the bed frame at a forty-five-degree angle to the floor. Captain Peña took one step and jumped onto the leg with his full weight. Victor's gorge rose at the sound it made and he nearly vomited. The boy was shrieking uncontrollably.

"You hear that, whore? You hear? This boy's leg is broken. That's what you've done. You've broken his leg. You could have stopped it, and you didn't. Next time you beg for mercy, I want you to think about what you did to this boy."

Tito kicked the boy in the head and the shrieks turned to moans.

"Put them together in her cell. Keep them both wet. Nobody gets any sleep until this bitch has told us everything she knows: brothers, sisters, grade school teachers, past lives, everything. This bitch is going to sing."

"Shit, boss," Tito grumbled, "I was hoping we could set the little faggot on fire."

"Maybe tomorrow." Captain Peña shrugged as he went out the door. "It all depends on the Virgin."

FOURTEEN

IT WAS NOT NECESSARY to torture the boy further; the woman was quite broken. The next day she sat across the table from Captain Peña and Victor and she told them everything they wanted to know.

And now it was over. The torture was done, the questions were done, it only remained to kill her.

It was nine o'clock, the night was black and violent. The sky had opened, and rain thundered around the little school in chestnut-sized drops that clattered on the hood and roof of the Jeep. The soldiers wore their plastic ponchos, beneath which their heavy arms bulged as if they were pregnant.

The woman was led—handcuffed, blindfolded, at gunpoint—to the Cherokee. The filthy tank top clung to her breasts, making the nipples stand out. Victor guided her into the back of the truck. The boy, unconscious and feverish, had to be carried. His pants were torn to the knee. A rough end of shin bone poked through the skin.

Even with the wipers flapping back and forth, the rain reduced visibility to a few yards, and Victor had to drive at a snail's pace. He knew the way to Puerto del Diablo—not because he had been there as a soldier, but because it was on Lake Ilopango, where he had gone swimming many times. Diablo was a high cliff east of the beaches where he had sunned himself as a teenager.

The windows fogged up and he had to slow down even more, wiping them off with the back of his hand. He was afraid that Tito, slouched in the seat beside him, would start to scream about not taking all night to get there. But nobody spoke. The atmosphere in the Jeep took on a thick, damp solemnity. The boy groaned whenever they went over a bump.

Victor could see Lopez in the rear-view. He wore an abstracted air, as if his mind were switched off. If Lopez felt any guilt about the murder he was about to assist in, the heavy features gave no clue.

They came to a sign that pointed to the public beach one way, Puerto del Diablo the other. Victor made a right, and they drove now in a slightly tenser silence.

"Stop here," Tito said.

"My name is Lorca," she had told them. Ten days of screams and tears had left her nearly voiceless. "Lorca Viera."

"Lorca? Lorca is not a first name. You want me to drag that boy in here and snap his arm too?"

"My name is Lorca," she said again, and Victor wrote it down. He was writing everything down. "My father loved very much the poetry of Federico García Lorca. He named me after this poet. It is a strange name, I agree."

"And this father of yours, tell us about him. Who is he? What does he do?"

"He's in his grave. He has been dead eight years. His name was Paul Nuñez-Viera."

"Oh, no. You have to be making this up. You are telling me your father was *General* Viera?"

"General Viera, yes."

"My God, I knew him! Isn't that amazing? I took a night-tactics class under him! General Viera! He was a wonderful soldier. A wonderful warrior! My God, you didn't mess with that man—he was one of the most intelligent, respected—can you really be related to him?"

The woman shrugged. "He was my father."

"Until the terrorists killed him. What a loss that was. What a catastrophe."

"For you, maybe. Not for the country. My father killed hundreds, maybe thousands of people. His death was a victory for El Salvador."

"You're disgusting. Your own father." The Captain asked about her mother then. Her mother was also dead.

"Will you get the boy a doctor?" she asked suddenly, catching the Captain off guard.

"Maybe we will get him a doctor. It depends how things go with you."

"The bone is through the skin. He will die of infection."

"Tell us more about your family."

Her relation to the famous general had changed the Captain's view of her, Victor saw. Even if she had hated her father, she could not deny the blood in her own veins, and the Captain was a great believer in blood. He spoke to her now as if they had struck up an acquaintance on a long train trip.

"You have a sister, do you not?"

"I have a younger sister. Teresa."

"Teresa works with you?"

"She works with me, yes. She helps feed the children at the church."

"Address, please."

She gave an address. Victor knew as he wrote it down that it would be the correct one. The sister would not be there now; the prisoner had won that battle. But she might be found eventually.

"But you don't just feed the children at the church, do you, Miss Viera. The food you were carrying was meant for the FMLN, wasn't it. Tell the truth, now. I really don't want to hurt that boy any more."

"Part of the food was for the children. The rest goes to the rebels."

"Thank you. Now we are making progress. Tell me how the schedules were arranged—we only caught you by accident, you know. It was just a random check."

She told the Captain what he wanted to know. The thin mouth, the drawn cheeks, her broken tooth—her features were a picture of exhaustion.

The questions went on. Coffee was brought, pads of paper were filled. The three of them took breaks and smoked cigarettes, Victor silent, Captain Peña chatting about inconsequential things. As the afternoon wore on, the Captain addressed the woman as if her own destruction had been a project they had worked on together—a tough job on the verge of completion—and now they could sit back and relax together.

He imagines that he has won, Victor said to himself, but this woman, this Lorca, has defeated us all. Because of her strength, the Captain and his men, all of us, have degraded ourselves. Her tank top is filthy, her face streaked with blood—the boy's, probably—and her hair is matted, but this woman is cleaner than we will ever be.

Victor's forearm cramped from scribbling all the things Lorca Viera told them. She told them how she dropped the food, a large box with a smaller box inside, at the church. She told them who sent her messages; his code name was all she knew, but she told them where she picked them up and the code names of those she relayed them to. More names, more addresses. So many addresses, but she had held out long enough that they would all be empty now.

Sometimes, as she paused to remember something, the tip of her tongue would touch the jagged edge of her front tooth. And then her words would emerge like small metallic objects, colourless and cold. All animation was gone from her, all passion, all hope, leaving just the voice, dry as blowing grass.

Even if we release her, Victor thought, this woman will be a ghost. Who could afford to be seen with her, a known detainee? What man would want her? It would be known she had been raped many times, and men had trouble forgiving the victims of rape. The woman had been extinguished. That was the object of the enterprise, he saw now, and they had achieved it. I have done that, he admitted to himself. I have done that to this woman because, unlike her, I am without courage.

"I believe you said earlier you have a brother," the Captain said. "Where is he, now? Is he with the rebels also?"

She shook her head.

"What was that? I didn't hear you."

"Miguel hid from the war. He went to law school in the United States. My father thought he would come back, but Miguel stayed there. I hated him for it, running from the war like that. He married a North American woman and he stayed. Now, I don't care. I am happy he is safe."

"Address, please."

"His office is on Seventh Avenue, I don't remember the exact address."

"We aren't about to pay him a visit, you know."

"I know. I did not write to him much. I don't remember the address."

"Home address?"

"I don't know. Some boulevard in New York City."

Victor's impressions of New York were shaped by movies. He imagined tall buildings, flowers, fountains, and beautifully dressed people.

Captain Peña circled back from family matters to her connection—slight though it was—to the rebels. Gradually, the gaps in her knowledge were established as consistent and thorough. After three or four hours it was clear she had nothing else to tell them.

"All right," the Captain said. "Thank you very much. Your troubles are over now. No more pain for you. Tonight we take you to Puerto del Diablo and shoot you."

"I see. Even though the President has been denying that Diablo is an execution site."

"Presidents have to be protected from some things."

"Why do you have to kill me?"

"You were aiding the rebels. It's called treason, and the punishment is death. It's simple justice."

"Then why are we all blindfolded? Justice does not hide its face."

"Don't lecture me, whore. I don't care who your father was."

"Will you let the boy go now? He has served his purpose, hasn't he?"

"I haven't decided yet about the boy. In any case, it's none of your business."

In the end, they took the boy with them. Tito had insisted. The boy had seen faces at the plantation; the sergeant could not risk the security of his men. More important, Victor knew they could not forgive the boy the evil they had done him. When he was safely dead, the wound they had inflicted on their own consciences would heal over.

"Stop here."

Victor pulled to the edge of the road and switched off the motor. Rain hammered at the Jeep and slid in sheets down the windshield.

"Please," the woman said. "I know my life is over. But don't kill the boy."

After her final interrogation, she had been no longer kept in solitary. She and the boy had been thrown in a cell shared by half a dozen others. Through the peephole, Victor had seen her comforting the boy, and she had repeatedly requested medical attention for him.

"You can let him live," she said now. "Surely you remember how young you were at thirteen?"

"Don't talk," Tito said—softly for him. Then he turned to Victor. "Listen, baby, you don't do a lot of the heavy work, do you?"

"Sergeant?"

"I just volunteered you. You take that bitch to the edge of the cliff and you kill her." Tito was pure force, his black eyes implacable. "Lopez, you do the boy. Well? What are you waiting for?"

Victor forgot to put up the hood of his poncho. Rain poured down his neck and into his shirt as he went around the back of the Jeep and opened the door. The woman stepped out of the Jeep without being pushed or pulled.

"Which way?" she said. "Let's get it over with."

He took her arm with absurd gentleness and led her the twenty paces to the edge of the cliff. The lake was hidden by curtains of rain, but he could hear the waves sloshing seventy-five feet below.

Victor took out his service pistol and pulled back the hammer.

"Mother of God," she said. "What are you waiting for!"

He stood behind her and raised the pistol to the back of her head. Her hair clung like seaweed to her small, round skull.

Ten yards away, Lopez leaned down and fired into the head of the prone boy. Once, twice. The rain absorbed the noise, making the shots sound like the tinny pops of a cap gun.

Victor's finger tightened on the trigger. The woman shifted her weight, and suddenly the mud gave way beneath her. The gun popped, there was a muzzle flash, and she was gone. Victor was frozen to the spot. He had missed her, he knew he had missed her. Shooting anything that close up, he would have felt the flash on his hand, but the gun had discharged into empty air.

The mud had collapsed beneath her just as he had fired. He did not hear her hit the rocks below. She was probably still alive. Had the others seen? Would they suspect?

Apparently not. They heard the shot, they saw her fall.

All the way back to town, Victor's hands trembled on the steering wheel. The rain clattered on the Jeep and reflected the headlights, all but blinding him. He nearly missed the turnoff that would take them back along the service road toward the little school.

PART TWO

Forgive me, if you are not living
If you, beloved, my love,
If you have died

—PABLO NERUDA

FIFTEEN

THE RAIN THAT FELL in New York City eighteen
months later was of an entirely different character. It
was March—the weather was gloomy and rainy—but
here the drops were tiny, as if they had been squeezed
through a sieve, and seemed to hover in the air rather
than to actually fall. This was not the driving natural
force of Victor's homeland, but a thin, dirty mist that
clung to his skin.

Living in the vast grey metropolis of New York was
like taking up residence inside a colossal machine. It
pressed, pulled, squashed, and stretched you without
regard for what you might choose or not choose to
do. In this one respect, it was not much different from
the army. Victor's feet seemed to carry him automat-
ically from the Thirty-fourth Street subway station and
through the impossible crowds outside Macy's. He had
thought about coming to this intersection with Seventh

Avenue—he had thought about nothing else for the past eighteen months—and yet he could not have said at what moment he had made the actual decision to do it.

Perhaps it was the time of year, with the last chill of winter still in the air, but the city planners of Manhattan seemed to have given no thought whatsoever to trees or flowers. Not in midtown, anyway. In every direction the vistas were grey, grey, grey—an endless monotone interrupted only by the hordes of lurid yellow taxicabs.

The address on Seventh Avenue was not at all what he had expected. The term "New York lawyer" had conjured in Victor's mind something far grander than this grubby building on this grubby corner. The plate glass of the front door was cracked, and the tiny vestibule smelt of urine. As Victor examined the roster of names peeling from the directory, his heart began to pound. One was a coward at all times and in all places, not just in wartime.

He remained poised before the directory with a sense of foreboding, the sense that he had been carried to this intersection, this building, as part of some cosmic plan, the sense that all his actions were now and always had been out of his control. The same feeling had engulfed him when he had faced the court martial. He had known from the first moment he had faced the tribunal—known with absolute certainty—that he would be found guilty, that he would be sentenced to death.

As Victor stood in the vestibule of this dirty building a world away from the little school, cowardice took hold of him once more. He turned from the roster of names and was pushing at the handle of the cracked front door when the elevator door rattled open behind him and a short, square man—a Mexican, Victor thought at first glance—came bustling out. He was wearing a rumpled shirt and tie and, seeing Victor, he clutched the tie nervously. "Are you by any chance Mr. Perez?"

Victor nodded. Perez was his name now; he had Ignacio Perez's birth certificate to prove it, and they had been close in age. That was why Victor had stolen his papers from the Captain's office. The actual Perez, he reasoned, was dead and buried and beyond caring.

"Mike Viera," the man said, giving him a handshake that was damp but firm. The resemblance was obvious; he had his sister's hollowed-out face, the same deep lines from nose to chin. "A thousand apologies. I hadn't forgotten about you, I was just dashing out for cigarettes. My receptionist called in sick today."

"I will come another time. When your receptionist is here."

"No, no, please. I'll be back instantly."

Viera spoke English so rapidly that Victor hadn't quite sorted out this last assurance until the lawyer was out the door. But he had no desire to converse in Spanish. Speaking English was part of being a new person; he had committed no crimes while speaking English. A new language was his best disguise.

Waiting for Viera to return, Victor stared at the chipped, discoloured tiles on the vestibule wall, the streaks on the elevator door where someone had tried to clean it with a dirty rag. He reread the names on the directory.

Viera came back, still apologizing. "I know I should quit, but I can't seem to get up the motivation. You smoke?" he asked hopefully, peeling Cellophane wrap from a pack of Player's.

Victor shook his head. I am Perez, he insisted to himself. Someday I will be Victor Peña again, when it is safe or when I have courage.

The sour smell of old cigarette smoke clung to everything in Viera's office. Along one wall, a row of dented green filing cabinets looked near to collapse. Some of the drawers hung open, others were missing entirely. An armless sofa sagged against another wall, its fake leather surface strewn with dog-eared file folders in several colours. Viera's metal desk was near the window but facing away from it. He sat behind it now and gestured at the couch. "Please, Mr. Perez. Have a seat."

Victor sat and stared at the lights of a peep show that flashed on and off beyond Viera's shoulder. *New York lawyer.* Where were the pinstripes and the wood-panelled office? Where was the wisecracking secretary? The alcoholic investigator? Next to the diplomas above the sofa hung a picture of Viera shaking hands with a slick-looking dignitary. Perhaps Seventh Avenue was a fall from earlier success.

"You wanted to talk about an immigration matter, I believe." Viera lit his cigarette and took a deep drag. "Is it for yourself?"

"Yes. I want to become a citizen. Or to get at least a green card." Even though the authenticity of the Perez documents was never questioned, Victor had suffered all the usual hardships of the illegal immigrant: the close calls with police or other officials who suddenly demanded identification, the search for affordable housing that turned into a search for an affordable slum, the long hunt for a job ever lower on the social scale. "If I can't become a citizen, a green card will do."

"It's twenty-five dollars for the initial consultation. Cash or money order is fine."

New York lawyer. Where was the expensive stationery? The discreet invoice? Mike Viera did not seem even a little embarrassed to state his fee, or that it was so low. Nor was he slow to accept the two crumpled tens and the five that Victor handed across the desk. He put them into his drawer, tore off a receipt, then resumed.

"Do you have any friends or family here? In the States, I mean, not just New York. Any relatives at all?"

"Relatives? No. Nobody. Well, I may know some people, but I haven't looked for them. No relatives."

"Is there anyone who can guarantee you won't become a burden to the state? Someone who will pay your way if you fail to get a job or become sick?"

"No. No one like that. But I already have a job, Mr. Viera, I can look after myself."

"We'll get to that. For now, the state doesn't care about facts, it cares about contingencies." Viera smiled, as if this were a very clever way of putting it. Perhaps he did not resemble his sister so much after all. He lacked her directness; he almost certainly lacked her strength.

"Well, there is no one to support me, no."

"That's bad. Now, tell me: you're not a doctor by any chance, are you?"

"A doctor?" Victor laughed. "No, I'm not a doctor."

"A physicist or a software designer?"

"No, no. Nothing like that." Victor had given his newly acquired background much thought. As an educated person of the middle class, he could never pass himself off to another Salvadoran as a peasant. But he stayed as close to the circumstances of the real Perez as possible. "I worked in the Department of Agriculture. It was my job to inform the campesinos of their rights under Land to the Tiller."

"So it's fair to say you are not an artist of stature? You are not about to produce letters saying you are a recognized artist? Or a writer?"

"No, I told you, I'm nothing. An administrator, maybe—not even an administrator. A social worker, maybe you could say."

"Forgive me, I did not mean to embarrass you. I have to ask these questions because Uncle Sam is very concerned that immigrants not take work away from American citizens. Certain categories of work—artists, doctors, the ones I mentioned—can be exceptions."

"But you also are from El Salvador, by your accent. How did *you* get to become a citizen?"

Viera stubbed out his cigarette. "My own case is not relevant." He sighed, stirring the ashtray with the tip of a pencil. "Unfortunately, Mr. Perez, the United States of America has no shortage of administrators or social workers. You say you have a job at this time?"

"Yes. I'm a chef's assistant. I make the salads at a French restaurant—Le Parisien." The owner was unpleasant and not even French, but it had taken over a month to find the job and he wasn't going to quit it now. "I also make the desserts. You should try my chocolate mousse sometime."

"Oh, my wife would never allow it," Viera said, and patted his pot-belly as if it were a lapdog.

"But what if . . ."

"What if what?" Viera said. "Go on."

"What if one were persecuted in one's home country? You know—a refugee. The United States gives sanctuary to refugees, I believe."

"Yes, it does. Cuban refugees are very welcome. Also refugees from North Korea or Cambodia. The United States is hostile to those countries and likes to embarrass them by accepting their refugees. The people of El Salvador, however, are another matter. The United States is on friendly terms with the government of El Salvador. Obviously, she could not be on friendly terms with a government that persecutes its own people. Therefore, there is no such thing as a political refugee from El Salvador."

Tell that to the real Perez, Victor thought, the dead Perez. "But . . . suppose you were tortured. Suppose you were held by the Guardia or the army and they tortured you. What if you could show scars?" His scalp wound. He could say they clubbed him.

"It makes no difference. There is no asylum for Salvadorans, period. Believe me, I wish it were otherwise. There are people I want to help, and I cannot." Viera lit another cigarette and regarded his client thoughtfully, assessing the damage his information had wrought. "Don't be too downcast. Perhaps you will fall in love and marry an American girl. That would solve all your problems. Notice, please, that I am not advising you to fake a marriage, or to pay someone to pretend to marry you. That would be illegal. All I am saying is that if you have a real marriage—a *real* marriage, notice—with an American citizen, you will get your green card and eventual citizenship. Short of such a marriage, however . . ."

"There's nothing I can do?"

Viera spoke more softly. "Don't take it so hard. People live here illegally for years. The INS does not come looking for individual immigrants. Even if someone were to telephone them tomorrow morning and say Ignacio Perez is in this country illegally, at such and such an address, they are not going to come banging down your doors to deport you. They are interested in sweatshops, factories—places that employ hundreds of illegals. Your job is a good place to be, Mr. Perez. Hang on to this job." Viera started folding papers and organizing files on his desk, signalling that the consultation was over. There were no other clients waiting, however. Finally he said, "Well, Mr. Perez—was there something else?"

"Yes. But I—I don't know how to say it."

"Take your time. Say what you want. It's what lawyers are for. We're a bit like priests, you know."

Victor took a deep breath. "I knew your sister in El Salvador."

"My sister." Viera's tone suddenly went cold. "Which sister?"

"Lorca, her name was. Lorca Viera. We were in jail together."

"If you are a fucking rebel, you can get out of here right now."

"No, no. I was not a revolutionary. Far from it. I told you, I was an administrator. But I was in the same jail as your sister."

"Well, then you know what happened to her."

"I thought they took her out and shot her. That's what they said. They said they took her out and shot her. But I heard—I heard a rumour that she was alive. Is it true?"

"Where did you hear this?" Viera asked sharply.

"It was just a rumour. Prisoners hear things from new prisoners."

"Bullshit. How do I know you're not from the Guardia yourself?"

"The Guardia—me?" Victor laughed.

"You said you worked for the government. Exactly what branch of the government?"

"Agriculture. I told you."

"Then tell me why—if you worked for the government—would you be a prisoner?" The lawyer in Viera came alive now, cross-examining him, badgering him even, but Victor had rehearsed his answers.

"Why was I a prisoner?" He looked Viera in the eye as he spoke. "I made the mistake of taking my job seriously."

"Meaning what, exactly?"

"In El Salvador, there is no land reform. For a campesino, to be given a deed of land is a death warrant."

"True. I have heard this." Viera sat back, looking Victor up and down, as if trying to judge his weight. "Frankly, Mr. Perez, I find it hard to believe you were in the same place as my sister. You are in much better condition."

"So she is alive, then. The rumour was true?"

"I did not say that," Viera said harshly, and turned away, clearly angry at himself.

"I understand," Victor said. "You are right to be careful." The Captain would have been proud of him for catching the lawyer out, but he felt a little ashamed. He had tripped a brother up in his love for his sister—where was the achievement in that?

As if to compensate for his lapse, Viera fired a volley of demands across his desk. "Describe the jail, please."

"It was a former school. A good one, built of brick. By missionaries, I believe."

"How many rooms?"

"Six cells, a guardroom, a kitchen, an office, I think. And the interrogation room."

"How many soldiers?"

"I believe only four. The squad was four soldiers and a captain. There were regular soldiers guarding the perimeter, but they never came inside, as far as I know."

"What was your cell like?"

"Concrete blocks. I think the cells were an addition to the school. Maybe six feet by four feet."

"How many prisoners?"

"I don't know. At least eight. There may have been many more."

"Where was it located?"

"The school? A little way west of San Salvador. Maybe fifteen miles."

"Very good, Mr. Perez. But prisoners were blindfolded at all times. How could you possibly know all these details—unless, of course, you were a guard, not a prisoner?"

A tremor went through Victor. "On my last day there, they took the blindfold off. Cleaned me up. Gave me new clothes. They used me in a show they set up, pretending to give away land. The press was there, everybody. They even promised me a deed, as if I had been working on a plantation or something. I knew what that meant. Several of the men I had helped to press such claims had been murdered. When I realized my job was a fake—worse than a fake, a trap—that's when I quit. And that's when they threw me in jail."

"If you were in that stinking place with my sister," Viera said, "kindly explain for me why you are in such good condition."

"Your sister suffered. Me, they just wanted to soften up for that show of reform."

Viera lit yet another cigarette, squinting at him through the smoke. "My sister never mentioned any Perez."

"We were not acquainted. Mostly I was in a cell across from her. She would not have known my name."

"How do you know her name?"

"Later, I was thrown into a cell with others. We whispered to each other. We promised that any of us who lived would contact the others' families. Do you know what it's like to know that your parents, your wife, your children, have no idea what happened to you? We promised to help each other this way."

"I see. Well, you had a bad time there, I'm sure."

"Everybody did. Your sister, though—your sister was brave."

"Is that some kind of joke? You think that's funny?"

"I would not joke about such a thing. Your sister suffered for days and days and told them nothing. All the prisoners knew this. She was the bravest person in that place."

"Really," Viera said. "Interesting." He lapsed into a silence.

Fine, Victor thought. Her brother doesn't want us to meet. That's fine. Victor had made his attempt to meet her, get to know her, somehow make amends. Few men would have done as much. Perhaps now the nightmares would stop. Perhaps now he could live his new life with a—if not a clear conscience, then a viable one. He rose to leave. "Thank you for your help on the immigration, Mr. Viera. Perhaps you will tell your sister that one who admires her courage was asking after her."

"What? Yes. Yes, of course. Goodbye. I'm sorry if I seemed hostile."

"It's nothing. One has to be careful."

The elevator—a tiny metal chamber much scarred with graffiti—was still open at the third floor. On the way down, Victor thought, That's the end of it. I wanted to try and set things right, but it's too much, pretending like that. I tried, and it's over.

A chill, damp wind was blowing when he got outside, but the rain had stopped. He turned uptown rather than face the Macy's crowds again.

He had to wait for a red light, and then a fire truck came screaming through, scattering cars and pedestrians before it. Then, as he was crossing Thirty-fifth Street, a voice called after him.

"Mr. Perez! Wait! Mr. Perez!"

He turned and saw Mike Viera hurrying after him. A cyclist swerved around the lawyer, cursing loudly.

"Mr. Perez. I'm so glad I caught you. Listen."

He had to wait for Viera to catch his breath. All those cigarettes.

"Mr. Perez," he managed at last. "Mr. Perez, I'm sure you don't want to relive those terrible days. But to be honest, I have long been hoping for something like this. An opportunity like this."

"Like what? What do you mean?"

"Someone who could help my sister. I've been hoping that someone who could help my sister would show up."

"Help her how?"

"Not help, exactly. Maybe not help. I don't know what I mean. Just—Mr. Perez, my sister needs someone who can understand what she has been through. Someone who knows what happened to her. She never talks about it. She refuses to talk about it. You would be doing a great kindness if you would come and see her. Frankly, she is not doing very well. She is not doing well at all."

"I don't know . . . Those days . . . I agree with your sister, in a way—to speak of those days is painful. One wants so much to forget."

"Yes, yes, it's understandable. Completely understandable. But don't you think it would help if she saw someone who knew exactly what she'd been through? What she's suffered? Sympathy is good, is it not? Come with me, just to say hello. It cannot hurt. It might help. Yes, I really think it might. Lorca is not doing well, Mr. Perez. She is not doing well at all."

That moment, as if a wheel somewhere deep beneath the concrete had once more been set in motion, Victor felt the sidewalk shift beneath his feet. Once more the implacable mechanism was set whirring, carrying him toward a future he could not avoid, even by changing his country, his language, his name.

"I'm not sure I understand," he said weakly. He could barely hear himself over the blaring horns, the squeal of brakes. "How could I help? What happened at that place, the little school, I cannot talk about it. No one can talk about it. I have nightmares all the time."

"So does my sister. She wakes up screaming. Sometimes she thinks she has been driven insane! But you seem so well, Mr. Perez. She needs to know this is possible. She needs to know things will get better."

"Yes, they will get better for her, I'm sure."

As suddenly as a child's, Viera's expression changed from eagerness to dismay. "You don't want to do it. All right, that's fine, I understand. I shouldn't have asked. A thousand apologies." Viera glanced at his watch. "And now I must be getting home. Good luck to you, sir."

"No, wait. Please." Victor grabbed at the lawyer's sleeve just as he was stepping off the curb. They were jostled by a man with a furled umbrella, then a woman on roller skates. They had to step back onto the sidewalk in the lee of a mailbox. "Of course I will come with you," Victor said. He could hardly keep his voice steady. "I would be honoured to meet your sister."

SIXTEEN

"DARLING! COME MEET OUR VISITOR! I have someone here who knows Lorca from El Salvador!"

Viera had driven him across town and through a tunnel to Queens and his home. Assessing the neighbourhood as they drove in, Victor had thought it displayed neither the power of a big city nor the quiet of a small town. The rows of houses had no cheer to them, the strip of ugly storefronts no charm. It was not a place anyone would *choose* to live.

A small blonde woman came out of the kitchen wiping her hands on a dishtowel. Helen Viera's face had once been pretty—perhaps not so long ago—but plumpness and unhappiness were rapidly claiming that territory. The eyes were cold as chips of Wedgwood, the corners of the mouth turned down in a near grimace. Victor had been expecting Mrs. Viera to be a Salvadoran, but she was American, though not from New York by her accent.

"Nice to meet you," she said, neither friendly nor hostile. "You're early," she said to her husband.

"My last appointment cancelled."

"Uh-huh. Was Alicia off sick again?"

"Yes. She sounded bad, though. I don't think she is faking."

"That girl's stealing your money, Michael. She's robbing you blind." The pale, puffy features broadcast unhappiness. It occurred to Victor that Helen was not just Viera's wife, she was Viera's green card, and years of dismay had been entailed in their transaction of marriage.

The lawyer's apparent cheerfulness increased in proportion to his wife's misery. "Helen, you remember we were saying how nice it would be if Lorca could meet someone who understands her difficulties? Mr. Perez knew her in El Salvador."

"Really? I'm not sure anyone can understand that sister of yours."

"But Mr. Perez was in the same jail," Viera said. "He was in the little school. I thought perhaps the connection—"

"You look a lot better than Lorca, that's for sure." Mrs. Viera was the second person to say so in as many hours. Would Lorca notice it too? "Dinner's ready in fifteen minutes," she added. "Will you be staying, Mr. Perez?"

"You are welcome to stay," Viera said. "I should have asked you before."

"Oh, no, no. I wouldn't want to be any trouble. Thank you, though. A thousand thanks." Victor's voice quavered, and he wondered if they heard. She was blindfolded, he told himself. She saw nothing. She cannot recognize me or my voice. I didn't utter more than half a dozen words in her presence.

"Darling, is Lorca upstairs?"

"Of course she's upstairs. Where else does she go?" Mrs. Viera retreated to the kitchen.

The house was a small semi-detached in Queens. The rooms were badly proportioned, the windows small. It was three times the size of the house Victor had grown up in, but far uglier.

"Lorca!" Viera called up a short flight of stairs that led straight off the living room. Victor followed him up the steps. "Come down, Lorca! You have a visitor!"

Sweat broke out on Victor's forehead; he had a sudden need for a bathroom. She was blindfolded, he reminded himself. She saw nothing. She cannot know my voice.

"Perhaps she didn't hear. We'll knock on her door."

The upstairs was tiny: two bedrooms, a bathroom, a closet. The hallway was narrow, the doors hollow-core. The clatter of plates from downstairs was audible, the sound of an oven door slamming; obviously, Lorca Viera would have heard her brother's call.

"Excuse me," Victor said. "Would you mind if I use your bathroom?"

"Of course not. Please."

In the bathroom, Victor's bowels moved quickly and forcibly. His relief was tempered with embarrassment, and he prayed that Lorca Viera would be out somewhere, that there would be no answer to her brother's continuous tapping on her door.

"Loud knocks frighten her," he said confidentially when Victor rejoined him. He leaned against the wood. "Lorca, there's a man to see you! A fellow prisoner from the jail . . ."

No sound from within.

"Lorca? Mr. Perez was kind enough to come all the way out to Queens. The least you can do is say hello."

"Maybe this was not a good idea," Victor said. "I should go, I think."

Viera shook his head, speaking insistently at the wooden door. "Lorca, dear. You have to see people sometime. You can't stay cooped up like a pigeon."

"Go away, Miguel. Leave me alone."

The ugly voice made Victor's heart shrivel. Memories crawled in his belly like worms.

"Lorca, please. Won't you at least say hello to Mr. Perez?"

"No. Leave me alone."

The wires, the dial, her screams. Suddenly Victor was terrified she would recognize his voice, even though he had said almost nothing to her. Even though it had been in Spanish. "I should not have come. No one wants to remember that place," he said, and backed toward the stairs. "I will go. You don't have to drive me, I will take the subway."

"No, no. You must stay for dinner."

"You're very kind. But it's better that I go." He started down the stairs. As he did so, the door was thrown open and Lorca Viera stood in the opening with black accusatory eyes. It was the first time he had seen her eyes.

"Where is this Mr. Perez?" She glared at him as if she would spit. The black eyes looked him over, taking in his cheap jacket, his wrinkled pants. "You were at the little school?" *Escualito.* She had unnerved him further by speaking in Spanish, though English was the language of this household.

"Yes," he answered in English. "I was at the little school. We never spoke. We were in different cells."

"There was a Perez there," she said in English. "They shot him."

Victor looked at his feet. "I heard the same about you."

"How could you even know my name?"

"Later I shared a cell with others. They told me your name. But they said you were shot."

"Unfortunately, I did not die."

"In my case, they shot the wrong man."

"Bravo. So what do you want from me? You want to fuck me or something?"

"Lorca . . ." her brother put in, but she went on bitterly.

"I got news for you, Mr. Perez. I was not raped in the little school, you know? So if you imagine maybe the guards fucked me so often I got a taste for it, you're wrong, okay?" She had begun to shake from head to foot. The claw-like hand was white and trembling where it gripped the edge of the door.

"Lorca, please," said her brother. "Mr. Perez only came to say hello. I asked him to come here. I thought you might talk to him. You don't talk to anyone else."

"But I did, Michael. I did talk, didn't I? I talked too much, if you recall. And because I talked, our little sister is dead." Once more she turned the black, excoriating eyes on Victor. "You some kind of vulture, is that it? You come to feed on what the guards left behind? Well, I'm not dead yet, Mr. Perez. Maybe when I am, my brother here will give you a call and you can come by and fuck the corpse."

She slammed the door in her brother's face. He looked down at the floor, shaking his head. "I have no words," he said. "No words to tell you how ashamed I am."

"It's all right," Victor said softly. "Your sister suffered a lot. She just wants to forget."

"I am deeply ashamed."

"Please, Mr. Viera. She just wants to forget."

Viera said nothing more until they were downstairs. "But that's the point," he said. "Lorca does not forget. She cannot forget. She stays in that room all day long and all she can think about is that terrible place you were in. She has to talk to someone about it. It's the only way she will ever truly forget."

"Did she even come out to say hello?" Helen Viera stood in the kitchen doorway clutching a salad bowl in one hand, a wooden fork in the other.

"It's okay," Viera said. "Lorca is not having a good day, that's all."

"Lorca's been having a bad day for going on two years, Michael. She was rude to you, wasn't she." The doughy, expectant face turned to Victor.

"It's all right. She suffered a lot."

"Yes. And doesn't she let us know it. Are you sure you won't stay for supper?"

"I am sure. Thank you very much, though."

Viera opened the door. "You understand, my sister didn't talk like this before the jail. This is anger, a reaction—well, it's true she was always angry, but not like this, not in this pointless way. Most days she won't even speak. She eats in her room. If you could have known her as a girl—she was so happy, so lively . . ."

"She has a lot of spirit. I am sure she was delightful."

"Mr. Perez, I don't know what to do. This is so hard on everyone." He tilted his head slightly toward the kitchen. "She has her good days, sometimes. Why don't you give me a phone number, and I will call you when she is feeling a little more—"

"But she doesn't want to know me. She said so very clearly."

"Sick people are often not interested in their cures. Please, will you let me call you? In return, I will refund your consultation fee." He pulled some bills from his pockets.

Victor tried to refuse the money, but the lawyer would not hear of it, pressing the bills into his hand. When Viera asked for his phone number, Victor gave him the number of the restaurant's pay phone.

SEVENTEEN

A WEEK AFTER THEY HAD DISPOSED of Lorca Viera, Captain Peña had taken Victor into the kitchen for what he called a cup of tea, although Victor had never seen his uncle drink tea. The Captain opened a pint of chocolate milk, which he gulped down with audible pleasure. Victor drank a Coke.

"Victor," Captain Peña had announced sonorously, as if from a pulpit. "Victor. They can say what they want of me when I am dead. They can say that Peña was an ugly bastard, they can say that Peña was a fool, they can say that Peña was too hard, too soft, too mediocre. I don't care."

"I'm sure no one will say those things, sir."

His uncle raised one hand to forestall contradiction and with the other wiped chocolate milk from his moustache. "The press, the army, the bureaucrats, they can say what they want—and they will, too, I know them. But one thing they cannot deny. What they cannot ever deny is that Captain Eduardo Vargas Peña—no matter what the situation—Captain Eduardo Vargas Peña stood by his family. Always he was loyal to his own."

A scream like tearing metal came from the interrogation room, where Tito was at work.

The Captain continued. "And as a man who always comes to the assistance of his family, I have—yet again, my underachieving nephew—I have yet again come to your rescue."

"How, Captain?"

"The United States of America is offering to train five hundred troops at Fort Benning, Georgia. Fort Benning, my boy! The School of the Americas! All of our best warriors have gone there, all of our toughest officers. Believe me, a course at the School of the Americas is a sure ladder to success in this army. And I—by pulling more strings than you can ever hope to count—I have managed to get your miserable carcass into it."

"You have? But that's wonderful, sir!"

"Ah, you are excited, I see."

Excited? Victor could barely suppress tears of joy.

"You have no idea," his uncle went on, "how difficult it was to secure this opportunity, given your sorry record. I had to call in every possible favour—some of them imaginary. I owe a lot of people now, on your account. You understand me? A lot of people. Well? You have nothing to say?"

"I'm overwhelmed, Captain. Truly. I don't know what to say."

"Let me down again, and I will man the firing squad myself."

"Oh, yes, Captain. Don't worry. I promise I will live up to the family name."

Another shriek from the interrogation room. A cheer went up from the tormentors, as if they had scored a goal.

Captain Peña drank the last of his chocolate milk and belched luxuriously. "You leave in two weeks. Make sure your papers are in order."

"I'll be ready, Captain. I promise."

The Captain stared at him in frank assessment. "Forget what I said about the firing squad. Tarnish the name of Peña, soldier, and I will personally hand you over to Sergeant Tito, you understand? I will tell the sergeant to be sure and take his time. I think Sergeant Tito would enjoy that." Captain Peña stepped out into the hall and, as if on cue, Tito tore from his victim's throat another scream.

Victor's transfer came in due time. But before he travelled to the United States, he removed from his uncle's files the identity papers of Ignacio Perez. The first night the visiting soldiers were allowed off the Fort Benning base, he caught a bus, and then a train, and then another bus, to New York City.

He had not planned to work in a restaurant, but he knew no one, and no other job was available. Le Parisien was located on East Fiftieth Street among a row of much better restaurants. Except for a trio of unpleasant waiters—all with identical moustaches—no one connected with the place was French. The owner was a shy, silent Greek who sat at his corner table sipping anxiously at a chain of espressos while his business sank inexorably into decline.

Victor worked a split shift, arriving at ten-thirty each morning and working through lunch, preparing salads and desserts until three. Then, after a two-hour break that he would spend sitting in a nearby branch of the New York Public Library, he would return to his station, little more than a stall really, and begin the dinner shift.

The French waiters said little to him, except to call him silly names when placing their orders. (Two profiteroles, *Potassio*. Three Caesar salads, *Ignoracio*.) They weren't hostile, exactly, they just assumed he was an idiot because he was Hispanic, and because a chef's helper compared to a professional waiter was a lowly thing.

The day after his trip to Queens, Victor took off his apron, raised the hinged countertop of his station, and walked out into the bright sunshine of Fiftieth Street. It was a cool spring afternoon.

Despite the chill, there were many people—clerks and secretaries, they looked like—seated on the steps of St. Patrick's Cathedral. They looked carefree, Victor thought as he ascended toward the great bronze doors. He had seen grand cathedrals in picture books and movies, of course, but St. Patrick's perfect neo-Gothic arches and beautifully carved saints were in stark contrast to San Salvador's national cathedral, with its facade of bullet holes. There the Guardia had fired into a crowd of protesters, killing thirty. No one took their ease on those steps.

The vast interior was dark and cool. Smells of candle wax and incense brought back childhood memories.

As a boy, Victor had revered priests as God's representatives on earth. But then the war came, and the army had taught him that priests were the enemy. The army hated the Church for many reasons. The teaching of history, with its catalogue of revolutions, they saw as subversive. And what need was there to learn of political systems less repressive than El Salvador's? But the priests ignored all warnings.

Archbishop Romero had written a letter to the President of the United States asking him not to send any more military aid. He told the President that military aid was used to slaughter civilians. Then he had preached a sermon telling soldiers they should disobey orders that were against the law—orders to abduct, orders to torture. The archbishop was shot the next day while saying Mass.

Such courage, Victor reflected, and I haven't even the courage to go to confession. He looked at the row of confessionals against the wall, where several penitents were lined up. He wanted to ask for forgiveness, he wanted to ask for advice, but he did not know American priests. He feared they might tell him to turn himself in.

He knelt in the back row and prayed for courage. If courage came, he would tell the priest about Labredo, about the boy. He would confess what he had done to Lorca Viera, and how he had intended to kill her, and how she had slipped at the crucial moment. If the courage came, he would tell everything, and maybe the priest would forgive him.

The courage didn't come. Victor went back to work with a leaden heart.

All through the dinner shift, the waiters called him ridiculous names. Then suddenly there was a panic when a party of eight all ordered Caesar salads at once. Nick, the lugubrious owner, had cheered up considerably and came into the kitchen to help. Later, there was shouting across the stoves as Fidel the chef threatened to kill a waiter who cancelled an order for filet mignon he had already prepared.

Fidel's Spanish curses echoing among the pots and pans were like an audio replay of the little school, and loathing swelled in Victor's chest at the sound. English was the language of sanctuary, of rebirth, of anonymity. In English, no one knew who and what he really was.

By ten o'clock, the orders stopped coming. By eleven, the place was empty. Victor put plastic wrap over the mousse and threw out the whipped cream. He washed his chopping block and the half-dozen knives he had used. Nick told him morosely that he could go home.

Fiftieth Street was quiet at this hour. The air smelt fresh after the kitchen smells of frying meat and hot oil. Maybe tonight there would be no nightmares. Victor stood at the top of the restaurant stairs, struggling with the zipper of his jacket. It was a cheaply made thing of fake leather he had found in a Salvation Army store, and the zipper always stuck.

"Just leaving, I see!" Mike Viera was grinning up at him from the sidewalk. "I was just passing through the neighbourhood, Ignacio. I'm so glad I caught you!"

EIGHTEEN

VIERA STOOD WITH HANDS IN POCKETS like a boy who is uncomfortable with his adult errand. "I thought I'd missed you."

"But you could have telephoned. I gave you the number the other day."

"A sudden inspiration. I was working late. Yes, very late. And then I was heading toward the bridge and I saw your restaurant and I thought, why not stop and say hello?" For a lawyer, Victor thought, Viera was a poor liar. "Tell me, Ignacio," he went on, "are you working on Sunday or are you free?"

"I'm free. The chef has a nephew who does my job on weekends."

"Ah, good. I was wondering, you see, if you would be so kind as to accompany my wife and myself on a picnic in Central Park. We go to the park often on Sundays—it's almost as good as going to the country. My sister

Lorca will be there too. She is enjoying one of her happier periods, it seems."

Far beneath his feet, deep in the white-hot caverns of the earth, Victor sensed a colossal grinding of gears. It was not over. "Your sister," he said, and coughed to cover the catch in his voice. "She is expecting me to come?"

"She knows I am asking you," Viera said, forgetting his tale of sudden inspiration.

"I don't know ... After the other day ..."

"Don't worry. She is in a much better mood, I promise you. Almost cheerful! You don't have to talk about the little school, you can talk about anything you like. It is just a picnic. Just good food and good company. We have every reason to expect a pleasant afternoon."

Victor looked up Fiftieth Street toward the traffic of Lexington Avenue. A taxi was blaring its horn at a bus stalled in the intersection. An ambulance went by, lights flashing. "All right," he said finally. "Should I bring anything? Some food? Something to drink?"

Viera beamed. "You will be our guest. Your presence alone will honour us."

Sunday broke fair—a crisp, clear day with fleets of white clouds chasing each other over the trees, a sharp wind gusting out of the north. Victor was glad of his windbreaker.

"Have more potato salad," Helen Viera urged him.

"Oh, no, thank you. It was wonderful, but I assure you I am quite stuffed."

"Nonsense." She dropped a large dollop onto his paper plate. "We'll just have to lug it home anyway."

"You're very kind. I seem to be eating everything in sight."

They were sitting on a blanket spread out on the bank of a small pond. Behind them, the newly seeded Great Lawn was an oval of pale emerald. A hill across the pond was guarded by a miniature castle topped with a fairy-tale turret. A spot for lovers, Victor thought.

"Another ham roll?"

"Oh, no. I couldn't."

"Men. You always say no when you mean yes."

"Don't force him to eat, Helen." Lorca was sitting under a tree, peeling bark from a stick. She didn't look at them when she spoke. She bent over the stick, shoulders hunched, her hair falling over her face.

"I'm hardly forcing him," Helen said.

"Believe me," Victor put in, "I don't have to be forced. This is the best meal I've had since I came to New York."

"See? He likes it." Mrs. Viera, who looked a tired thirty, spoke in the hyper-dramatic tones of a twelve-year-old.

Lorca stood up, brushing twigs from her jeans. She walked down to the edge of the water. Victor was still afraid that she would recognize him—some catch in his voice, perhaps even his smell—and suddenly know with certainty what he had done to her. She had barely glanced at him for the past hour, but he was still afraid.

"Finishing off the food, I see." Mike Viera was coming toward them from the washrooms.

"I gave him the last of the potato salad," his wife said, snapping a Tupperware lid shut. "Lorca didn't like it."

Viera was wearing jeans and a green striped polo shirt, and looked ten years younger than he did in his lawyer suit. He snatched up a Frisbee and yelled to his sister, "Lorca! Catch!"

She turned from the pond just in time for the Frisbee to catch her in the chest. Victor expected an angry outburst, but she just retrieved it from the mud and tossed it back without a word. The Frisbee cruised toward her brother in a perfect arc. Viera threw it back. "We used to play for hours when we were kids," he said to Victor. "Flying saucers, she used to call it. Never wanted to stop." The Frisbee sailed over a low-hanging branch into his hand. "Let's move away from the water. Come on, Ignacio."

Victor had not played at anything since he was a boy. The game of catch seemed foolish. And he had a faint sense of rudeness that Helen Viera was not invited to join in. She sat alone on the plaid blanket, reading a novel by Danielle Steel.

He was completely uncoordinated at first. He threw the plastic disc too hard; it soared over Lorca's head and she had to run after it. Then, in a single motion, she swung around and sent it curving toward her brother. Viera was businesslike, dispatching the toy toward Victor's grasp with the neatness of a fact.

As the game progressed, Victor became more skilful. It even became easy. If only speech were this easy, he thought. If only trust and friendship could be so natural.

"This was a good idea," he called to Viera. "To bring this thing along."

"For a picnic, a Frisbee is essential. You didn't know this?"

Viera whipped it straight and level, chest-high to Victor. Then Victor launched it into a graceful tilting flight to Lorca. She had only to take one step, a short leap, to pluck it out of the air. In that swift, clean motion she looked perfect, Victor thought. Undamaged.

"You two continue," Viera said. "I am fat and middle-aged and require my rest."

"Lazy!" Lorca yelled after him. "Lazy old man!" She stamped her foot in a comical way. Then she spoke to Victor for the first time that day. "You've had enough too, I suppose. You want to join the little old man? The senior citizen?"

Victor shook his head, holding out his hand for the Frisbee. With a flick of her wrist, Lorca sent the bright plastic disc whizzing into his palm. As they played on, his technique continued to improve. He could now place the Frisbee pretty much where he wanted to. Yes, he thought, I'm like a normal person now. I'm doing a normal thing.

Despite the cool breeze, he worked up a sweat. Several times he thought surely Lorca would have had enough, but they played on and on. How could this leaping, grace-ful girl be the hunched and bitter woman of an hour ago?

The clouds arranged themselves into high-banked columns of cumulus that now and then hid the sun. Victor and Lorca played in shade then sun, shade then sun. It got windier, it got colder, but they played on, Lorca silent and serious, Victor sometimes shouting "Good throw!" or "Sorry!"

No one would ever know what I did to this woman, he thought. She may even come to like me. Is this what being good feels like? This ease, this freedom, is this how the brave feel every minute, every hour? With me, of course, it is a performance, and all performances have their final curtain.

"It was the same when we were children," Viera said when they joined him and his wife on the blanket. "Lorca never wanted to stop. She would have played in the pitch-dark."

"Why not?" Lorca said, accepting a plastic cup of lemonade from Helen. "They make ones that shine in the dark, you know. They are called—I forget the word for it, this shining."

"Phosphorescent."

"Phosphorescent." The word came out with a slight whistle, and she covered her mouth with her hand.

"We should get that tooth fixed," her brother said. "It makes you look like a street person."

The tip of her tongue probed at the tooth. She turned away and stared at the water. "I am cold now."

"Because you're sweating," Helen said. "I told you to bring a jacket. Tell her she's foolish, Ignacio."

Victor said nothing. At the mention of Lorca's injury, shame had coiled itself around his chest. He could hardly breathe.

They didn't stay long after that. The plates and napkins were thrown in the trash, the Thermos and blanket packed away.

"This is the happiest I've seen her," Viera said as they headed back across the park toward Fifth Avenue, "the happiest since she came here. This is how she used to be, Ignacio. So easy and free. Not this anger all the time, this rage."

Lorca had been walking ahead of them, but she stopped at the edge of the park drive, where cyclists and roller skaters whooshed by. She said, "I think I would like those, the Rollerblades. I would like to try that sometime."

"You would fall and break your head," Viera teased her.

"I would not. Helen, you want to learn?"

Viera's wife looked surprised that she had been addressed. She stammered a little. "Gosh, I don't know. Skating is for children, isn't it?"

"It's not a crime. Grown men and women are still in part children."

"Oh, that's a lot of hogwash. I don't believe that for one second."

But Lorca did not hear. In a swift change of expression, her mouth opened—the broken tooth a sudden black triangle. She was staring beyond Helen's shoulder at something on the road.

Victor followed her gaze.

Coming up the hill, lumbering amid the throngs of skaters and bicyclists, was a green Jeep Grand Cherokee. The windows were tinted, the driver and passengers nothing more than dark shapes. A terrible trembling shook Victor in the knees. It's going to stop, he thought. It's going to stop and Sergeant Tito will jump out and arrest me.

"What's wrong?" someone was saying.

It's just a Jeep, he told himself, a recreational vehicle. They're everywhere. But his legs trembled all the same.

Lorca ran.

Viera and Helen turned on the path, gaping after her.

"It's the truck," Victor managed to say. "The Jeep. It's what the Guardia drive."

"Good God," Helen said. "Where the hell's she going? Does she expect us to go and pry her out of the bushes?"

"We can't just leave her," Viera said. "She doesn't know the park. She might get lost."

"Michael, Lorca is a grown woman."

Lorca had rounded the pond. She vanished among the trees below Belvedere Castle.

"I will go," Victor said.

"You'd better not," Helen said. "You don't know her moods."

But Victor was already hurrying toward the pond. The trees were not yet in full bloom; dark figures moved among winding paths. As Victor entered the darkness of the Rambles, a ball of fur scuttled out from the bushes trailing a red leash. Victor nearly tripped headlong. "Sorry," a young woman called to him. "Scampy, you come back here right now."

He stopped at the crest of a small hill. Below him on one side, cars rushed across the Seventy-ninth Street transverse; above him on the other, laughing children ran around the castle.

"Lorca?" he called. "Lorca, where are you?" A couple walking hand in hand parted to let him pass. "Excuse me," he said to the man, "did you see a young woman run in here? Dark hair? This tall?" He held his hand, palm down, about five feet off the ground.

The man shook his head and started to walk on, but the woman pointed down the hill they had just climbed. "There was a woman by herself, near the water."

"Water?"

"By the willow trees. She was wearing blue jeans and a loose blue shirt."

Victor thanked them and hurried on. He had to clamber down some rocks to reach the waterside path. The willows were visible from the far side of the tiny lake where youngsters and tourists rowed rented boats. Their fronds trailed over the banks and into the water.

As he came around the curve of the hill, he could see a flicker of blue between the emerald branches. "Don't be afraid," he said in Spanish, forgetting his fear for the moment. "No one will harm you here."

There was a shuffling sound from the willow; the blue disappeared.

"Please don't run," he said softly. "There is nothing to run from."

Silence from the willow. Distant laughter from the lake. From farther off, the barking of a dog.

"The truck," he said. "I know it frightened you. It frightened me too. It's just like the ones the Guardia drive—the tinted windows, everything. Believe me, I know them well."

Two men came around the hill holding hands. They glanced at Victor talking to the tree, but were too engrossed in each other to remark on it or laugh.

"The tinted windows," Victor pressed on. "They like them, the Guardia, because they know it is frightening to be watched by someone you cannot see."

Not a word from the willow. From the water, the creak and splash of oars.

"You know why else they like those dark windows? They like them because they are cowards." *Cobardes.* He spat the word.

"English, please."

The reply was so faint, the words so unexpected, that Victor was not sure he had heard correctly. "Pardon me?"

"Speak English. I hate the sound of Spanish now. To me, it is an obscenity."

"You?" he said in English. "Named after a fine Spanish poet, you can disown your language?"

"It is a good word, *disown.* I disown everything. If I could, I would disown myself."

Victor knew all about that. He longed to disown

Victor Peña body and soul, not just his name. But probably only death could do that.

"I prefer English now." Lorca's harsh voice, with its cracks and hoarse texture, emerged from the tree as if from a confessional. "It feels . . . it feels so far away." She said *far away* as if it were a quality of great and rare beauty.

"Yes. It does feel far away. I am still not used to it."

A pause. Then, from the tree: "You are a good person, aren't you."

"I am not," he said. "I am not a good person."

"You are a good person," she repeated in a factual tone. "It is obvious you are. I, however, am not."

"No, no," Victor started to say, but she shushed him.

"Let me say it, Ignacio. I thought at one time that I was a good person. I imagine every person on earth thinks that he or she is good. A little bit good. I thought that I was good and kind. I thought that I was generous. I even thought that I was brave. Now I know otherwise—that I am none of those things. And sometimes this knowledge is hard to bear."

"It is not knowledge, Lorca. It is anger and disappointment. I feel those things too. I feel them about myself. About things I have done. Things that happened at the little school."

"People are dead because of me. Because I talked. It would have been better if they had really shot me on that cliff. It was just sheer luck that cliff gave way beneath me."

"That's how you survived? The cliff gave way? Where was this?"

"Diablo. The middle of a storm. Hard, hard rain. Suddenly a mudslide, and I nearly drowned. It would have been better if I had."

The rain and the wind came back to Victor. The distant roar of the sea, and the dead boy. It was me, he imagined saying. That was me, behind you with the gun. But he could not face her hatred. "You blame yourself," he said. "But no one else blames you. At the little school, you were known as the bravest."

"Known how? By who? Prisoners were not allowed to speak."

"We whispered together, as you know. When we spoke of you, it was only in admiration."

"You are mocking me."

"I swear, Lorca. Even the guards. I heard two of them talking one day. They said you were the toughest."

He pulled the fronds aside and stepped into the cool, dark space within. Lorca shrank from him, pressing her knees into her chest. She was trembling all over, though whether from the cold and damp beneath the willow or still with fear, Victor could not be sure.

We are like lovers in here, he thought. Only a lover should be with a woman in such a dark, secluded space. He reached tentatively toward her shoulder, but drew back when she looked up at him.

"I told them where my sister lived, and now she is dead. You understand me?" Her eyes overflowed, but she did not allow herself the relief of real weeping. "She is *dead*."

Victor murmured in a low monotone that was almost prayer, "They beat you, and you did not speak. Shocked you, and you did not break. Half drowned you, and you spit in their faces. Even they raped you, and you said nothing."

"Raped me." She looked at him with sudden ferocity. "Who told you they raped me?"

Victor stammered. "I'm sorry. I didn't mean—"

"This is a lie. This is the guards' lies. They did not rape me. Beat me, yes. Everything else, yes. But rape me, no. They did not rape me."

"But you said they did. The other day."

"No, I said they did *not*. You think they would lower themselves to do this? You think they would dirty themselves? Contaminate themselves with a guerrilla bitch? Never. You hear me? Never."

"I am sorry. I should have thought before I spoke."

"You imagine I would still be alive if they had raped me? I would hang myself from the nearest tree. I would have shot my brains out."

"I am so sorry. Please forgive me." She had turned her back on him, and Victor cursed himself for a fool. Rape, he suddenly realized, was the most lasting torment the little school had inflicted on this woman. The pain of the shocks may have receded, the bruises from the beatings healed, but she would go on and on being a woman who had been raped, and that knowledge was too much for her. "Please forgive me," he said again.

"I am in no position to forgive anyone," she said. "Even if I wanted to."

"Lorca! Ignacio, where are you?" Michael Viera's voice came from behind and above them.

Lorca hid her face against her knees. Victor stepped out from the willow. Viera looked down at him from halfway up the hill.

"She is here with me," Victor said. "We are coming now."

"Let's hurry, please, Ignacio. It's starting to rain."

In the shelter of the willow, they had not noticed the rain. By the time they rejoined Helen, who was waiting for them on a bench near the Obelisk, the sky had turned charcoal.

"Did you have a nice time?" Helen asked Lorca brightly. "Enjoy your little walk? We had a dandy time wondering where you were."

"Leave her alone," Viera said. "Let's get to the subway before we get soaked."

Lorca was silent. As the others said goodbye, she scuffed at the dirt with her shoe. Victor watched them pick their way through the diehard skaters, Viera carrying the basket in one hand and guiding his wife with the other. Lorca kept her distance from them and moved in a careful, hunched posture, bent as if over a wound.

NINETEEN

VICTOR TOLD HIMSELF he wanted no contact with the Viera family for a while. He stayed away for the next few weeks, working his split shifts at Le Parisien, spending his breaks in the library or sometimes in a cheap coffee shop with a newspaper, trying to distract himself from thoughts of Lorca.

His home, if you could call it that, was a rundown SRO hotel on West Ninety-fourth Street, one of the last of these crumbling hostelries on the upper West Side. It was a shabby, depressing place. Victor had a hot plate in his room, a small sink, a wobbly iron bed and peeling wallpaper. The bathroom was along a dingy hallway. Half the time the light didn't work, and even though Victor had twice scrubbed the place himself, the tub and sink were always filthy.

The Royal Court Hotel, as it was grandly named, was an hour's walk from the restaurant. To save money,

Victor walked it every day, despite almost constant rain.

One wet day, he stopped beside the Belvedere fountain in the middle of Central Park. The rental boats were stacked up onshore; the lake was empty except for a squadron of ducks paddling toward the iron bridge. Victor stood at the water's edge and stared across the lake at the willows where he had talked with Lorca. He stood there for quite a while.

That was three weeks after the picnic. A Sunday.

The following week, as he was cutting through the park one night on his way home after work, he strode purposefully past the fountain with its wide-winged angel. He had resolved before entering the park that he would not stop there, he wouldn't think about Lorca.

One glance, however—what could that hurt? A single glance could not do any harm. And so Victor allowed himself this single glance across the lake and kept moving. But then he rounded the bottom of the lake and noticed a waterside gazebo. A moment later he was sitting on a bench inside the gazebo, and telling himself he would stay just five minutes. Five minutes to enjoy the moonlight rippling on the water, the satin glow of the lamps among the trees.

He stayed for over an hour.

When he rose to leave, his legs were damp and stiff. I'm like a man who haunts the scene of his crime, he thought. But that was not quite accurate, because his crimes against Lorca had been committed in another country.

Later, as he lay in his narrow, tumorous bed at the Royal Court, he could not remember what he had been thinking for that hour. What had passed through his mind as he stared across the water? What were his thoughts as he gazed at the moonlight on the willows? He could not remember. He remembered Lorca's trembling shoulders and her broken tooth. He remembered her harsh voice and her unshed tears.

Victor switched on his ceiling light, tugging on a length of string he had rigged above his bed for the purpose. He reached under his mattress and extracted from among the bedsprings a wristwatch. It was a Bulova heavy with features he did not understand, dials within dials. He read the inscription on the back: *To M. from J.*

He switched off the light.

The watch dial glowed in the dark.

"I am sorry."

The loudness of his own voice startled him.

"I am sorry," he repeated more softly.

The dial glowed as if he held a part of Lorca's life throbbing in his hand. Maybe it would be all right to call the Vieras, an inner voice suggested. Nothing wrong with that. Just to see what they're up to, he told himself.

Just to see how she's doing.

TWENTY

VICTOR STOPPED BY Mike Viera's office unannounced. He was surprised to see Lorca sitting behind the receptionist's desk. She was busy on the phone, and Viera's door was closed. Victor sat in the tiny waiting area and watched her over top of a *Sports Illustrated*. She was arranging a meeting between Viera and another attorney, speaking quietly into the phone. Instead of her usual faded jeans and work shirt, she was dressed in a neatly pressed blouse and skirt. Except for the chipped tooth, she looked like any other professional New Yorker. Should I ask her now, he wondered? Or is it too soon?

"The Frisbee champion," she said when she hung up. "How are you?"

"I am very well, Miss Viera. How are you?"

She shrugged. "My brother has chosen to enslave me."

"You look like you've been doing this all your life. Very professional."

Before he could say anything more, the office door swung open and a woman came out. She was perhaps thirty, with heavy eyebrows that gave her a sad appearance. Her complexion was pebbled from burnt-out acne. She said to Lorca, "I have to see him again next week. I have to bring my mother."

Lorca reached for a calendar. Mike Viera waved for Victor to enter.

"Come in! Come in, Ignacio! What a pleasant surprise," he said, shutting the door behind them. "I wanted to ask you to come to dinner next week. I was afraid after Lorca's distressing episode in the park we would never see you again." He gestured for Victor to sit on the couch.

"I enjoyed our picnic," Victor said. "It was a wonderful afternoon."

"So you'll come for dinner on Saturday?"

"I would like to, very much."

"Good. It's settled. Eight o'clock."

"Eight o'clock, Saturday." Yes, he thought. I should ask her now.

Victor sat down on the vinyl sofa, and a stack of files slid to the floor. He knelt and tried to balance the files into a loose pile against the wall.

"Leave them, Ignacio. It's nothing. Tell me how you like my new receptionist. The old one called in sick too often."

"It looks like you have a perfect arrangement now."

Viera emptied a full ashtray into the wastebasket and lit himself a cigarette. He took a drag and contemplated the stream of smoke as he exhaled. "To be honest, I am already a little regretting my decision to hire Lorca. She scares the clients, I think." Viera stared up at the ceiling, as if debating whether he should go on.

"But she looked like she was doing very well to me."

"Today is a good day. Three days ago it was a different story. At home, maybe nine o'clock, I go to ask her something and I can't find her anywhere. I look in the basement, I look in the garage, even in the crawl space above the garage. Finally, you know where I found her? Under the bed. She was hiding under her bed, shaking like a leaf. Some boys had been letting off firecrackers on the street."

"At the little school, the first thing they do is destroy your nerves. Stop you sleeping. Scream at you all the time. It makes the interrogation worse."

"It makes *life* worse."

"They frighten me also, firecrackers. It sounds like the war."

There was a silence. Viera stubbed out his cigarette. "My sister used to call me a coward. You too must think I'm a coward for running away from that war."

"I am no judge of cowards. Only a madman would run *to* that war."

"Hah! You are a subversive, Ignacio."

"No. Nothing like that."

Viera sighed and swivelled to look at the hideous view of Seventh Avenue behind him. "Lorca has told me very little of what they did to her at the little school, but I am not blind. Did you notice the scars on her arms? And that tooth? You know some stinking guard punched her in the face? That's how that tooth was broken. Can you imagine, Ignacio? Can you imagine yourself ever, under any circumstances, punching a woman in the face?"

No, he wanted to scream. *But I was terrified. They would have killed me.*

"I am not a violent man, but if I had before me the man who did this to my sister, I would kill him."

"I would not blame you." Suddenly Victor needed to be anywhere but this office.

"School. What an obscenity, to call that place a school." Viera swivelled back to face him again. "Well, I don't have to tell you. They must have done terrible things to you also in that place."

Victor got up and in his nervousness managed to knock another stack of files to the floor. "I had better get back to work before I destroy your entire place. And someone has to make chocolate mousse for the rich, no?"

"Wait. Please, Ignacio. I'm trying to find . . ." Viera was shuffling through papers on his desk, lifting up files, clipboard, legal pads. "Here it is." He snatched up a creased yellow brochure and thrust it across the desk. "Have you ever heard of this place?"

Victor read the front of the brochure. *You are not alone,* it said. *If you have been abducted, detained, physically maltreated, or tortured, the Torture Victims Association can help you.*

Viera said, "I finally talked Lorca into going. She practically spit in my face the first time I suggested it. 'A bunch of crybabies,' she called it. But you know, even after only a few meetings, it seems to be doing her a lot of good."

"She talks to these people?"

"They are victims, the same as her. Same as you. People who were jailed and beaten and God knows what. It does them good to talk, I believe. To know they are not alone. And Lorca has decided she likes very much the man who runs the place. Bob, I think his name is. Bob something."

Victor was surprised by a pang of jealousy.

"I thought maybe you would like to go, Ignacio. To talk to these people. You might benefit from it too."

"Me? I don't think so, Michael. It's very kind of you, but I don't need such a place." The chance of being recognized was too great. Someone who knew the real Perez. No, no, he could not consider it, even though it meant passing up a chance to get closer to Lorca.

"Think about it. Lorca is getting better—you noticed the change yourself."

"Goddamnit!" Someone was shouting in the outer office.

Viera, followed by Victor, got up to see what was going on.

His client was standing in the middle of the reception area, clutching her arm. "Goddamnit!" she said again. "I don't believe this place!"

"What is it? What's wrong?"

"She hit me. Your goddamn receptionist hit me, that's what's wrong."

Lorca was gone.

"Are you all right?" Viera said. "Let me see."

The woman took her coat off and showed him her upper arm.

"There's no bruise," Viera said. "Please sit down for a moment and tell me what happened."

"I will find Lorca," Victor said.

He took the stairs down to the street. He searched through the crowds, stepped into two coffee shops and a McDonald's, but she was not there. He stopped into a laundromat, a liquor store, even a psychic's storefront. Not finding her, he finally gave up and went back to Viera's office, passing the outraged client as she left the building.

Viera was staring forlornly out at the avenue.

"Did she tell you what happened, your client?"

"She says all she did, she asked to use the phone. To see if she could get off work a certain day. It took her a while to get through, and Lorca asked for the phone back. My client asked her to wait a minute and Lorca lost her temper. Her nerves are so bad, Ignacio. She has no patience at all."

"I'm sure she'll get better. It's a matter of time, that's all."

"Delay of any kind—the slightest wait for anything— it makes her crazy. Absolutely crazy."

"At the little school, they would make the prisoners wait. It was part of the punishment. They would sit a prisoner in that room and just make them wait and wait, knowing what was going to happen. But not when."

"I don't know what to do, Ignacio. I am her brother, but there is only so much I can do. Already, it is putting a strain on my marriage. My business too, if this keeps up. This has cost me a client. That woman is not coming back, you know. I don't blame her, either."

"It's hard for you, I know. You are very good to your sister."

"She hates being so dependent on me. I know she hates it—it hurts her pride, although she doesn't say so. You'll still come for dinner on Saturday?"

"Yes, of course."

"Thank you. She needs a friend, Ignacio. Not a relative, a friend. Someone she can trust, someone she can respect."

"I would be happy to be that friend, Michael. Except your sister has no reason to respect me."

"Oh, you are wrong. You know what she said the day we went to the park? She and Helen had a fight on the way home, they're always fighting. Later, I went up to Lorca's room. I wanted to tell her about this support place." He held up the yellow brochure. "I was telling her about it and saying how it might speed her recovery. And you know what she said? She said, 'I know you want me to be like Ignacio Perez, but I cannot. I could never be strong like he is.' That's what she said."

"I am not strong," Victor said. It was all he could think of to say, and he repeated it. "I am not strong at all." He felt an ashen grief that Lorca could be so deceived. It's as if I go on and on tormenting her, he thought. As if I cannot stop.

TWENTY-ONE

A COUPLE OF DAYS EARLIER, Victor had made a discovery. One of the waiters at Le Parisien had told him of a three-dollar cinema not far from the restaurant. Victor had assumed such a cheap place would be down-at-heels and depressing. He imagined holes in the movie screen, broken seats, a floor tacky with chewing gum. So he was first surprised, then disbelieving, when the theatre turned out to be a grand place with deep blue carpeting and huge screens. He had never set foot in such a beautiful theatre.

Full of excitement, he purchased a ticket for a science fiction movie, even though he would have to leave before the end to get back for his second shift. The film had a great many explosions and truly revolting wormlike aliens, and Victor enjoyed it immensely. Then came a scene where an unlucky earthling was immobilized upon a table and the aliens did something to him that made him scream and scream. If he lived in the world portrayed in the movie, Victor would be numbered among those alien worms, not among human beings. Clearly, he couldn't take Lorca to a movie like this. Perhaps a romantic story or a comedy, she might enjoy one of those.

He had wanted to ask her at Viera's office. Before his discovery of the three-dollar theatre he had not thought he could afford such an extravagance. His pay as a kitchen helper was barely above minimum wage, and the cost of taking a woman to the movies was staggering: after Coke and popcorn you were looking at twenty dollars or more.

But the fantasy had stayed with him and flowered into detail over the following days. Victor saw himself sitting next to Lorca in the darkened theatre, saw the two of them laughing at amusing antics onscreen, felt her fingers brush against his in the popcorn bag. Reflections from the screen cast a silvery glow on Lorca's hair, and when Victor reached for her hand, she gave his an answering squeeze.

But three dollars. She might think he valued her cheaply. She might think he had no class. Of course, she didn't have to know it cost only three dollars. He could buy the tickets ahead of time and maybe distract her a little as they entered.

Saturday night, eight o'clock. For once, Victor was grateful that the chef's nephew worked Saturday nights.

He arrived at the Viera house on the dot of eight. Lorca greeted him at the door, wearing a long patterned skirt and a deep red blouse that was very flattering.

"Ignacio," she said. "You are so good to come when I have been so awful. I'm very glad you're here." Her attire was so colourful, her manner so bright, that Victor's mood changed immediately from apprehension to confidence.

Viera was in the living room, watching a baseball game. He bounced out of his chair and clicked off the TV the moment Victor came in. "Just in time for a beer, Ignacio. I was about to pour one for myself. Come in, come in, make yourself at home."

Victor followed him into the kitchen, where Helen Viera was chopping vegetables and tossing them into a pot. "Well, well, it's our goodwill ambassador from El Salvador," she said. "This is an honour."

Victor couldn't be sure if she was making fun of him, but perhaps that edgy feeling came from the *clack, clack, clack* of her knife. "It smells wonderful, Helen. I hope this is good enough to go with it." He handed her a bottle of wine. The man in the store had assured him it would be appropriate with just about anything.

"Oh, we're humble folk here," Helen said. "I'm sure it will be more than adequate."

Viera took the bottle and examined the label. "*Graves.* Oh, yes, this is a very good wine. We should uncork it now and let it breathe."

Viera busied himself searching for a corkscrew. Lorca reached into the fridge and opened a beer, handing it to Victor. "He's forgotten you. Miguel's head can contain only one thought at a time."

"*Huh*," said Helen. "Just what you want in a lawyer."

"It means he's at least honest, Helen. More lawyers should be like him."

"Lawyers aren't paid to be honest."

"You hear how they talk about me?" Viera said in the tone of the beleaguered man of the house. "If I can manage this without breaking the cork, it will be my biggest achievement of the day." The corkscrew was a complicated tool with arms that lifted like wings as Viera twisted it. After much careful but noisy manoeuvring, he managed to extract the cork. "Hah! Success!" He sniffed the mouth of the bottle. "Oh, yes. We shall enjoy this."

Helen Viera shook her head, the corners of her mouth turning white. Victor saw how Viera's relentless cheer could grate. Was it natural to him? Or had he learned it as a counter to his wife's attitude, to Lorca's high-voltage outbursts? Of the responses available to a man at close quarters with such women, relentless cheer may well have been the best.

Helen shooed them out of the kitchen, and they sat in the living room in a sudden shy silence. This Viera rushed to fill with a not very interesting story about an immigration officer who had been found to be corrupt. Lorca sat staring into her drink, swirling her glass slowly as if she had lost something in it.

"I wonder where Bob is," Viera said when the room was once again silent. "Lorca? Did you hear me?"

"I'm sorry. What did you say, Miguel?"

"*Michael*," he corrected her. "I said I wonder where Bob is."

"I don't know."

"Who is Bob?" Victor asked brightly, as if the prospect of meeting someone with that name were a particularly happy one. In fact, he was a little deflated to learn he was not the Vieras' only guest.

"Bob?" Viera said. "Bob runs the support group Lorca goes to. I haven't met him yet, but I hear only good things. Tell Ignacio about him, Lorca."

Lorca didn't look up.

"Lorca? Can you tell Ignacio a little about him?"

"I don't want to right now." Her voice, so cheerful just moments ago, was now husky with dismay, as if she were ashamed of having been happy.

"Oh, come on, little sister, cheer up."

Victor stared at his shoes, which he had spent a long time polishing. They were second-hand—all his clothes were second-hand, sifted from the musty counters of Salvation Army outlets—and the shoes pinched his feet. He wanted to take them off, but then they would see the holes in his socks.

The doorbell rang and Lorca sprang up to answer it. The next few moments, when Victor recalled them later, were a mosaic of discordant images: Lorca flying to the door, a red blur in her rush to answer it, the door opening, and a broad, ungainly man with a profuse brown beard taking up the entire living room, booming out greetings, shrugging off an overcoat the size of a tarp. He shook first Viera's hand, then Victor's, squeezing his fingers in one hairy fist, gripping his bicep with the other. *Comrade!* the gesture seemed to say. *Courage!*

"Bob Wyatt!" he boomed. "Glad to know you, Ignacio!" Then, turning with an uptilt of the beard and a ferocious sniffing: "Oh, something smells fabulous! Who's in the kitchen! Who's in that kitchen cooking up a storm! There's some culinary artist doing very creative things in there, and I want to meet her." He seemed to be everywhere at once, the great smooth boulder of his back turning this way and that, like a bear's. Now he was in the kitchen booming out compliments to Helen before he'd even been introduced. "Bob Wyatt! Lorca's friend from TVA! Great to meet you! Boy, this is a treat for me! I'm the worst cook in the state! I spend my life in restaurants—if you can call 'em that—places run by guys named Aristotle and Cosmos. Terrible!"

Victor had never met such a loud man; not even his uncle was so loud. Confidence blasted from every inch of him—from the heroic bush of his beard to the size-thirteen cowboy boots on his feet. And that wall-shaking voice, somewhere between trombone and timpani.

"How was your trip to Washington?" Lorca asked when he was settled into a chair with a beer.

"Splendid!" he cried. "Absolutely splendid! *Tick, tack, tock!* Everything turned over like clockwork. I wish every meeting went that well. I could retire and go fishing!"

Victor pictured him catching a salmon in his great paw.

"What were you doing in Washington?" Viera asked.

"Groundwork. Project we've got coming up. You know about the certification hearings? Aid to El Salvador?"

"A little. Military aid, right?"

"Right. Every six months the administration has to satisfy Congress that El Salvador's making progress in land reform and human rights. If they fail, that's fifty million dollars the El Salvador military doesn't get."

"It's not the President who decides?"

"Nope. It's the Appropriations Subcommittee of the House Foreign Relations Committee." The words rolled easily off his tongue, as if the corridors of power were his home address.

"You sound like you know your way around," Viera said. "You go there a lot?"

"Nah. Not anymore. Used to. Used to be an organizer."

"Organizer?" The English word was a new one to Victor.

"Labour organizer. Political side. Getting people out to vote. Believe me, it was just as glamorous as it sounds. I was working the phones night and day."

Behind him, two sliding doors parted and Helen Viera appeared. "Dinner's ready," she said. "What are you all talking about? Everyone looks so serious."

"Just politics," her husband said. "Nothing you have to worry about."

Helen's face hardened at this brush-off, and Victor felt a sudden sympathy for her. She was the outsider in the family, not Lorca. "Don't let it get cold," she said, and retreated to the kitchen.

Viera rose. "Gentlemen, we have our orders."

They seated themselves around the dining room table while Lorca and Helen brought in the food. There was baked ham, corn on the cob, mashed potatoes and some other vegetables Victor didn't recognize.

"Tremendous!" Bob shouted. "Absolutely tremendous, Helen!"

He would be the kind who always remembers people's names—also the kind to use the first name on first meeting. But even Helen slowly warmed under the onslaught of his bonhomie.

The wine was poured, they clinked glasses, and then the next few minutes were filled with the passing of dishes and jokes about how much Viera and Bob put on their plates, and how little Lorca put on hers.

"You couldn't keep a rabbit alive on that," Bob said. "Six, seven days, you'd have one dead bunny."

"Oh, Lorca has to make her little points," Helen said.

Bob smiled, ducked his head to his wineglass to avoid the sudden chill. His bearish hide was apparently not too thick to sense female hostility.

"I am not making any point," Lorca said. "I am simply eating what I can. It's not to make any point."

"Sure, Lorca. I believe you."

"Why do you say such things? The meal is good, and now you accuse me of something."

"Good wine," Viera said. "Good choice, Ignacio."

Victor felt his cheeks redden.

"God, I meant to bring some wine myself," Wyatt said. "Left it too late, and then the damn store was closed. The one near me, anyway."

"Don't think about it. We have plenty to drink," Viera said. "But these Appropriations people—the committee. You talked to them in Washington?"

"God, no. Not the committee. The hearings aren't till June. But I want them to know we're coming." He took a sip of wine, his ease implying that Bob Wyatt was a force to be reckoned with around Capitol Hill. "I've been hustling administrative assistants, smoothing the way for people from TVA—people like Lorca, if she'll come—to testify at the hearings."

"I will never do this," Lorca said quietly.

"Testify?" Victor's heart was racing. "A person could get killed, testifying against the military. The Guardia is not going to let—how much? fifty million dollars?—get away without doing anything to stop it."

"I understand your concern, Ignacio, believe me I do. It's not unfounded. But the fact is, you're not in El Salvador anymore. You're in the United States. We do some bad things around the world, real bad things. God knows, we have a habit of backing the wrong people. But in our own yard? Different story. They're not going to let anything happen to any witnesses. No, sir."

"I am sorry to disagree with you. The Guardia will not stand by and do nothing. I know them. They will not let such hearings take place. Such testimony."

"They've already taken place, Ignacio. They've held three of these hearings over the past eighteen months. True, it hasn't stopped any actual military aid. Not yet. The hearings are loaded with so-called experts from the State Department. Those guys will lie through their teeth to get what they want, they'll say anything. Anything! They get up there and testify that the number of killings has gone down since the last hearing. That the number of disappearances has gone down. And actually, they usually have—just prior to the hearings. I mean, they're not *stupid* down there. And the only people testifying from the other side are organizations like Amnesty. I mean, bless their hearts and all, I love those people, but they just roll in with their own facts and figures and it's like, believe the expert of your choice."

"And you want Lorca to testify."

"I will not," she said.

"Oh, not just Lorca. I want every Salvadoran I can find. Every man, woman and child whose rights were abused down there. We have three Salvadorans in our group. One of them witnessed a massacre in her village—horrific story, horrific—and another had to watch while her husband was set on fire right before her eyes. They broke his legs and set him on fire, can you imagine?" He put his fork down with a clank. "Oh, I'm sorry. I'm spoiling this wonderful meal with this stuff."

Lorca was not even picking at her food now.

Victor tried to change the subject. "They say the Yankees have a good chance to win the pennant this year. What do you think of the team so far?"

"Oh, sports," Helen said. "I don't know what's worse—torture or sports."

Victor rifled through the contents of his mind to come up with another topic. But Wyatt, chomping his food and gulping his wine, got in ahead of him. "God, that's good ham, Helen. I haven't had ham that good since some faraway Easter of my youth. But let me just say one thing—" Now he tipped his great bulk toward Viera and Victor. It was like being addressed by a mountain. "Just let me say that if I can get those two to testify—those two women I mentioned—and *Lorca*," he added with heavy emphasis, "it'll toss one big fat monkey wrench into the works of that committee, you bet it will. They won't be able to ignore testimony like that. Call me an optimistic fool, but I think we can stop that military aid. I think we can stop it on the fifty-yard line."

"They will not let Lorca testify," Victor said. "Or any of the others. They will not. You don't know them."

"All right. You're raising a cogent point there, Ignacio. Very cogent. Part of the reason for my trip to D.C. was to organize security. You would not believe the red tape that involved. It all has to be approved by the State Department, of course."

"The State Department? But you said the State Department favours the military. They provide the liars and experts, no?"

BREAKING LORCA | 193

"The State Department employs twenty thousand souls, Ignacio. Not all of them have a stake in seeing your country ruled by a gang of thugs. I *assure* you, every precaution will be taken to ensure the security of our witnesses."

"Perhaps Ignacio should testify," Viera said. "Did you know he was a prisoner in the same place as Lorca?"

"That so-called school?" Bob turned to Victor and laid a heavy hand on his forearm. "Well, damn, Ignacio. Maybe you should trundle on down to TVA sometime. Come with Lorca one night."

"Oh, I don't think so. I just want to forget."

"Can we *please* stop talking about torture and murder and the military," Helen said. "I mean, there is a limit. There really is."

"Okay, that's it. That's all," Bob said, holding up his hand like a traffic cop. "Our Blessed Lady of the Table has spoken, and I for one have no intention of violating her wishes." For the next twenty minutes or so, Bob devoted himself to getting back into Helen's good graces. He suggested she think about teaching a cooking course at night school, probed her about her childhood in Minneapolis, asked if she had any sisters as attractive as her. My God, Victor thought, you may be dangerously naive, but you sure are a first-class politician.

Viera, too, appreciated his efforts, as men do whose wives are difficult. The lawyer became relaxed and thoughtful—something he could not do when straining to surround everyone in good humour. Gradually Bob steered the conversation back to Washington, and Helen was so charmed she pretended not to notice.

Wyatt told them which congressmen were on the committee, who was likely to vote in what direction, and what other organizations would be likely to produce witnesses. His enthusiasm and absolute belief in the justice of his cause were hard to resist. Lorca eyed him with furtive admiration, and Victor felt a good deal of admiration himself. But as Wyatt talked on, a familiar sense of dread spread inside him like ink. The powerful presence of the man, his booming voice, his big gesticulations—even though he was a vastly different person from Captain Peña—Victor felt a similar loss of control in his presence. Once again, one fate was being sideswiped by another.

Apple pie was brought in, eliciting another fountain of hyperbole from Wyatt. Once or twice Lorca smiled at Wyatt's remarks, flashing her broken tooth then dipping her head to conceal it. Victor felt the sting of jealousy. Yes, she really admired this man, perhaps even had a crush on him. It would not be a good time to ask her to the movies; Wyatt completely dominated the room.

This was Victor's fantasy as they sat on at the table: If Bob did not interfere, he would gradually become closer and closer to Lorca. Eventually, he would apologize to her for the hideous things he had done to her. He would get down on his knees and beg her forgiveness. And, all things being possible in fantasy, she would forgive him. Just imagining such a moment sent a thrill of relief through him.

And then? Well, his fantasy grew cloudy beyond that point. But things were going well between him and Lorca. Things were going very well, and there was every chance that eventually . . . But now this half-trained grizzly beside him was diverting the flow of events into another direction entirely: Washington, congressional hearings, sworn testimony. It boded ill for Victor, very ill, and he said a fervent prayer for Wyatt's non-existence.

TWENTY-TWO

VICTOR WORKED OUT A PLAN to ask Lorca the question that he had never got to ask last time. He had been rehearsing it over and over in his head ever since. He would arrive at her brother's office—casually, as if he had just happened to be in the area, shopping at Macy's . . .

"But where are your packages?" Lorca demanded, when he was standing in front of her desk. She was slotting files into a battered cabinet. Victor was alone with her for once; her brother was in court. "You go all the way to Macy's and you don't buy anything?"

"I was looking for—looking for jeans." Nervousness made him stammer. "They didn't have my size. They were sold out, unfortunately."

"You are so fat, is that it? They don't keep those gigantic sizes?" She spoke without looking at him, slamming one drawer shut and opening another.

"My problem is the opposite," Victor went on, trying

for a jaunty tone. "A thirty-two waist is very common. They sell out of this size very—"

Lorca answered the phone, informing a caller that her brother was in court and would not be available until tomorrow. She went back to her filing, and Victor tried to think of something else to say, but he was too nervous, alone with her like this.

Lorca had trouble closing the bottom file drawer. She yanked at it, and suddenly the whole drawer came free, crashing onto the floor, sending files slithering. She kicked at the cabinet, swearing violently in Spanish.

Victor knelt to pick up the drawer. He had to stack the files neatly on a couple of chairs first. Lorca was leaning back against the wall, covering her eyes with one hand.

"Objects," he said quietly. "Objects can drive a person crazy sometimes." He leaned past her to stack some files. He could feel the heat of high emotion from her skin. He fetched her some water, rinsing out her coffee cup at the drinking fountain down the hall. "Go on, take it."

She took the cup from him with a distracted scowl, as if she had never seen such a mug before. Tears shone on her face. He handed her a Kleenex from a small box on the desk, and waited a few moments until she seemed calmer.

"I know it's not a good time now, Lorca. You're upset. But I wondered if you would like to go with me to a movie this Saturday. A comedy called *Fat Tuesday.*"

"No." She took a sip of her water, put the mug down. She tore another Kleenex from the box.

"All right. Okay. Maybe another time. Maybe when you're feeling better."

"I'm never going to feel better, Ignacio. This is how I am. I used to be a strong person, you know? Not anymore. Now, a file cabinet can make me cry like a baby. That's what I am. I am not going to feel better. Don't waste your time on me. I don't know why you would, anyway."

"I thought you might enjoy seeing a movie. And I would enjoy your company."

"Go away, Ignacio. You don't want to know a person like me. I am not a person. I am a ghost."

Victor walked to the door. He stood there for a moment with his hand on the knob. Finally he said, "I too was sentenced to death once, Lorca. I too was saved at the last minute. Why shouldn't two ghosts see a movie together? Maybe together we would make up a whole person."

"Please, Ignacio. Just leave me alone."

"The movie is at six-thirty, if you change your mind. The corner of Eighth Avenue and Fiftieth Street. Not far from here."

That was Wednesday. For the rest of the week Victor consoled himself with the thought that it was the file cabinet Lorca had been angry with, not him. Her tone with him had been—not angry, exactly—but weary. He even began to hope that she might show up at the theatre, and Saturday afternoon found him in his room at the Royal Court worrying about what he should wear.

He selected a tapered, dark brown shirt with white piping on the collar, cuffs and pockets. He had found it at the Salvation Army for five dollars—five dollars, brand new, still in the package—and a week later he had bought himself a pair of white trousers at the same place. Together, set off with a wide belt and brass buckle (also from the Salvation Army), they made him look pretty sharp.

He showered, shaved for the second time that day, and polished his shoes even though he had worn dime-sized holes in them.

He dawdled on his way down Broadway, stopping at the curbside displays of books and magazines. At one of these he examined a Louis L'Amour novel with an interesting cover. A young couple were leafing through art books at the other end of the table. They looked almost like twins: both wore white T-shirts and denim shorts, both were blond, both wore sunglasses. There was a suggestion of opulence about them. As they walked past him, the young man said, "Did you see that guy's shirt?"

"I know," the woman answered. "Straight out of the rodeo."

Victor examined his reflection in a store window. That white piping everywhere—he should have realized. Only a fool would buy such a shirt. No wonder it was in the Salvation Army. Someone with better taste had got rid of it.

Lorca must see in him the same simple-minded wetback those gringos saw. He'd been kidding himself;

there was no chance she would show up. A scattering of fat raindrops smacked onto the pavement, and Victor quickened his pace. To get soaked on top of everything else, that would complete the ruin of his Saturday.

As he neared the theatre, he saw Lorca coming from the opposite direction. Despite the clouds, she was wearing dark sunglasses that hid her eyes completely. Below the sunglasses, the sharp downward turn of her mouth was almost a caricature of anger. She looked like she was going to kill someone.

Victor hurried to buy the tickets so that she wouldn't see how cheap they were. Then he waved at her and Lorca hurried toward him—responding, as always, without the faintest trace of a smile. To make her laugh, Victor thought, now that would be a real victory.

"I have tickets," he said, holding them up. "We can go right in." He hurried her past the box office to the escalator. "So, you changed your mind after all. I'm glad you did."

No smile. Just a glum nod.

Her silence felt like an accusation. "You want some popcorn? Something to drink?"

"No. Nothing."

As they took their seats, Victor couldn't think of a thing to say. Perhaps his shirt was to blame for her mood. Maybe she was embarrassed to be seen with him. He asked her what was the last movie she saw.

"I don't remember. It was years ago. I was a little girl. I don't go to movies."

I should have thought of something else for us to do, he scolded himself, she hates movies.

The feature turned out to be a funny story about a man who believes, erroneously, that his wife is cheating on him. His jealousy drives him to ever more idiotic lengths—first to preserve his wife's virtue, then to prove her false. One scene, involving an expensive restaurant and a mouse, had the audience howling with laughter. And yet, on Lorca's face, there was not a flicker of a smile.

"Do you want to leave?" he whispered. "We can go, if you want. We don't have to stay."

Lorca just scowled and kept her gaze on the screen. His own enjoyment withered, the way it had with the shirt. Suddenly the trumped-up situations onscreen, the exaggerated faces, seemed juvenile, trivial, not remotely funny.

"I am sorry you hated it," he said when it was over and they were heading through the lobby. "I thought it would be funny, but it wasn't funny at all. Not after the beginning."

Lorca shrugged. "I thought it was funny."

"You did? But you didn't laugh once. You didn't even smile."

"I don't, Ignacio. Not anymore."

They came out onto Fiftieth Street and turned east toward Eighth Avenue. Rain hung in the air in a fine mizzle, and Victor felt water seep into his shoes. As they waited for the traffic light to change, Lorca said, "It's wonderful the movie only cost three dollars."

202 | GILES BLUNT

Victor was plunged into gloom. They walked the next long block in silence. When they reached the subway entrance, Lorca touched his arm. "You are angry with me?"

"No, I am not angry with you."

"Yes, you are." The injured, disapproving eyes searched his. "Is it because I mentioned the three dollars? You're embarrassed about this?"

"I'm just feeling quiet now, that's all. Look at him," he said desperately, pointing to a black man playing an electric guitar across the street.

But Lorca would not be distracted. "Why, Ignacio? You think I would like this movie better if it cost more money? I assure you, the opposite is true." She grabbed his arm, squeezing hard. "You were smart to discover such a place. I am glad you took me there."

Her gravity only increased his mortification. He wanted to dive into a manhole.

"It's much better to be careful with money than to throw it away. It's the difference between a husband and a clown." She let go of his arm. "There. That's the most conversation I've had with anyone since I left El Salvador. That's good, yes? See, Ignacio? You're very good for me."

"Good for you? I just seem to upset you."

"Everything upsets me. I can't help it. Everything *hurts*, Ignacio. I'm always on the edge of crying or screaming— every minute of every day. It's as if they peeled my skin off in that place. All my nerves are exposed."

I'm sorry. The words rose to his throat and choked him. "I wish I—" He broke off.

"Wish you what? What do you wish?"

"I wish—I understood you better."

"What is there to understand? There is nothing. I went to a school where they taught me how weak I am. How pathetic. How small. How afraid. Perhaps you learned something else in that school."

"No. No, Lorca, I learned exactly the same things." He looked away from her, toward the hurrying crowds on Broadway.

"But I feel better around you, Ignacio." She pulled at his sleeve until he faced her again. "Maybe because you were there too. I know you understand. And that makes me feel better. So you *are* good for me, you see?"

"You really think so?"

"*You really think so?*" she mocked him, too harshly for it to be funny. "Yes, I think so. Even if you are so stupid."

The rain had started up again. Pedestrians pushed by, cursing, hurrying down the subway stairs.

"Listen, are you in a hurry to go home?"

"Oh, yes. I miss my sister-in-law so much when I am not there."

"You want to go somewhere cheerful and cheap for a Coca-Cola?"

"No, Ignacio. I would rather stay here and get soaking wet."

TWENTY-THREE

THEY WENT TO A McDONALD's, where they shared a Coke and french fries and talked for two hours, nearly three.

They talked about the strange and frightening city they had moved to—though not nearly as frightening as San Salvador. They talked of their experiences in North America: the confusing manner of the gringos—alternately so warm and then so cold—that made trust difficult, friendship impossible. They talked about the native Hispanics who seemed to look down on Latin people not born in the United States. They talked about the angry stares of store clerks when comprehension was not immediate. The sensation of complete mutual understanding was new to Victor, and it thrilled him.

When they stood once more at the top of the subway steps, the rain had stopped and a warm breeze blew out of the south, tossing Lorca's hair into a tangle. "The air feels so good now," she said. "So clean and fresh."

Victor leaned close to kiss her.

"No," she said, and with a sudden movement pushed him away. "I don't want to be kissed." Then she turned and hurried away from him down the subway stairs, her quick, light steps echoing after.

For days, Victor felt the imprint of her hand on his chest with a mixture of shame and anger. A kiss would have felt like forgiveness. I am in love with her, he told himself tentatively, testing the words.

He stood in front of the pay phone for a full half-hour before he managed to put a coin in.

"No, not a movie this time," she said. "There is somewhere special I would like to take you."

"Special? Special how? Where do you mean?"

"Don't panic, Ignacio. It's not expensive, and you don't have to get dressed up."

"But tell me what it is."

"You will see." That was all she would tell him, despite his repeated entreaties. "You will see soon enough."

He asked her yet again when they met up, outside a doughnut shop in Penn Station. Victor had arrived twenty minutes early and had worked himself into a state of high anxiety by the time Lorca got there. She had taken some trouble over her appearance; she was wearing makeup and a light perfume. She smiled upon seeing him, and yet again he was shaken by the black spark of her broken tooth.

"Tell me now. Where is this secret place you are dragging me to?"

"It's a church."

"A church? You want to go to church on a Saturday night?"

"A special church. You will see when we get there."

It certainly didn't look special. Our Lady of the Assumption was hidden in a shabby block of West Thirtieth Street. The structure had once been white limestone, but a hundred and twenty years of New York soot clung to the facade in a black film. In a niche by the side entrance, a statue of the Blessed Virgin spread her arms in welcome, though one of her hands had been snapped off at the wrist.

Lorca opened the side door and waved him in.

The basement was all curling linoleum and water-stained walls. Alcoholics Anonymous posters hung next to childish drawings illustrating the alphabet. Another poster showed a cute little old lady raising her fist above the words, *Seniors, Rock the Vote!* A battered aluminum urn was set up on a trestle table, and the place stank of burnt coffee.

Seven or eight people slouched uncomfortably in rows of metal folding chairs. They were mostly women, all Hispanic, and Victor suddenly realized with panic where he was. "Lorca, no. I don't want to be here."

"I didn't either, Ignacio. Not at first. But it has helped me a lot."

"I cannot. It's too much. I don't know any of these people."

Lorca took his hand and towed him toward the chairs,

but he pulled away. She shook her head. "Really, Ignacio, there's nothing to be afraid of. Why should you be so scared?"

Because somebody might recognize me, he wanted to scream.

"Everyone is afraid the first time. Just sit quietly. No one is going to bother you." She took his hand in both of hers. "Please stay, Ignacio. Won't you stay with me?"

There were only eight people in the place, and none of them looked familiar. My hair was shorter then, he told himself. And I wore a uniform—at least, until I joined the special squad I wore a uniform. Civilians see only the rifle, the sunglasses. They don't see your face. I don't look like a soldier now.

A voice boomed out across the basement. "Ignacio! You made it! Good going, Lorca!" Bob Wyatt's massive frame blocked the doorway, and then he was rolling toward them, hand extended. "Glad you could come."

"He is not happy about being here," Lorca said. "He wants to run away."

"Oh, everyone wants to run away the first time." Wyatt squeezed Victor by the shoulders and eased him down toward a chair. "Sit down, sit down, take a load off! Just relax and you'll be fine."

Wyatt's entrance had caused a stir. The others in the room had turned to look at them. One woman—a Salvadoran by her heavy features—was staring with intensity at Victor. The man beside her whispered something to her, but she kept her eyes fixed on Victor.

"Evening, all! Sorry I'm late!" Wyatt strode up to the makeshift stage, waving a sheaf of papers. "Some preliminary announcements!" he hollered, and launched into a list of scheduled events that meant nothing to Victor, until he got to the matter they had discussed at the Vieras'. "The congressional hearings are just two weeks away. We need more witnesses. Remember: nothing but good can come of testifying—good for you, good for your country, good for my country."

"Not so good if you end up dead," a man with a patch over his eye commented wryly.

"True. That would be a negative thing. But you don't have to worry about that. I've checked out the security arrangements myself. You'll be completely safe. Any more volunteers tonight?" He aimed his beard first at one side of the room then the other, but there were no takers. Lorca stared resolutely at the ceiling. "Well, all right. No one's going to force you, that's for sure."

"I know who you are." The accusation shot across the room like an arrow. Victor had no doubt who had said it, and to whom. The woman was still staring at him with black, venomous eyes.

She had spoken in Spanish, and Victor answered her in Spanish. "Well, I don't know you."

"You were not a prisoner. You were a soldier."

"Hold on a second, there," Wyatt said. "Can we just finish with the announcements first?"

"I was not a soldier. I was an administrator in land reform."

"You were with the Guardia. You came to our village. You killed people."

"It was not me. I was never a soldier." A thick sweat had broken out on Victor's brow. *They can tell. All of them know.*

"Please, Yvonne," the woman's husband said. "Leave the man alone."

"I will not. He is Guardia."

"Why would a soldier come to be among people like us?" he asked her gently. "I am sorry, sir," he said to Victor. "My wife was mistreated by the Guardia. For this reason, now, she sees them everywhere. Even in the United States."

"I am not mistaken! I have seen this man in uniform! He came to our village in Chalatenango!"

Victor had never been to Chalatenango. "I was not a soldier. I was a prisoner."

"You don't have to defend yourself to this woman," Lorca said softly.

"They came in the middle of the night," Victor continued. "They took me to this place, blindfolded—always I was blindfolded. I get there and the Captain kicks me." He pointed to his crotch. "Kicks me harder than I have ever been kicked in my life."

"If you were blindfolded," the woman said, "how do you know he was a captain?"

"I don't know. Someone called him Captain. I don't want to talk about this."

"Of course you don't," the woman said. "Because

nothing you say is true. If you were a prisoner, tell us what jail you were in. Tell us what they did to you."

"It used to be a school. A little school. They threw me in a cell by myself. They fed me meals full of salt, meals full of bugs. They stopped me sleeping. Day and night, they threw buckets of cold water on me."

"It's true," Lorca said to the room at large. "This is exactly how it works at the little school. I was treated exactly this way."

"You know this man? You were at the same place?"

"I was with him in the little school. What he says is true. It is exactly how they treat new prisoners."

"Oh, yes? What else did they do to you, then?" The woman shook off her husband's restraining hand. "No, let the poor suffering prisoner tell us himself."

"I told you, I don't want to talk about it."

"Hold on, hold on." Bob Wyatt put his hand up for order. "Nobody is forced to talk here. Ever. I don't care who it is. Many of you were forced to talk in the past, and that is the last thing we want going on in this group."

The woman shrugged. "A convenient arrangement if you happen to be a soldier."

"Don't say that again," Lorca warned the woman.

"Mother of God, I'll tell you what they did to me." Victor leapt up. "They played Submarine with me, all right? That's what they did. Held me underwater in a tank full of shit. Does that make you happy? They beat me on the head. Here, you want to see the scar?" Victor bent forward to show the woman the crooked white scar at his hairline. He found there were tears in his eyes. "They shocked me with wires. Put wires on my fingers, my teeth, my ears—and here." He pointed again to his crotch.

"You don't have to talk," Wyatt put in again. "No one here has to talk against his will."

But Victor couldn't stop. It was as if real memories were flooding through him. "Over and over they would shock me. Over and over they would say, 'You ready to play ball now? You ready to play ball?' Over and over they would say this, and apply the electricity. It felt like an earthquake in my flesh. It felt as if my flesh split open to the bone."

There were scattered murmurs of recognition among the crowd. Lorca had covered her mouth with her hand.

"You think you will not cry," Victor went on, weeping openly now, "and you do nothing but cry. You think you will not scream, and you do nothing but scream. I would have told them anything. Anything they wanted. But all they wanted was for me to play a part in this ceremony— a big ceremony in front of the Presidential Palace. 'See! This is land reform! We are giving all these men a piece of land!'"

"So they tortured you," Bob Wyatt said, "to make sure you wouldn't give the game away?"

"And because I had encouraged others to apply for deeds under the law. They said they would bring me my own deed within the next few days. I knew what that meant."

"What did it mean?"

"They come and kill you," the man with the patch over his eye said. "I knew of a man who was killed this way. The Guardia showed up in the middle of the night and shot him in front of his wife and children, then they stuffed the deed in his mouth."

"God," Wyatt said. "The committee needs to hear about this." He produced a box of Kleenex from somewhere and held it out to Victor.

The woman who had made the accusation was sulking now, arms folded tightly across her chest. Victor was astonished at the lies he had told, the amount of detail. He had not planned it. It was as if sheer wanting to have been on Lorca's side had convinced him it was so.

Lorca was looking at him, her mouth open a little and an expression in her scorched-out eyes that Victor had never seen before.

"You think you did something wrong, don't you," Wyatt said. "You think by playing along with them, by playing their game, you committed a terrible evil."

"I did," Victor said bitterly. "It was a terrible evil. You don't know."

"No, Ignacio. You did nothing wrong. Nothing. It's the people who did these things to you—the Guardia— they are the evil ones. Not you."

Around the room, pale, shaken faces nodded agreement. As Victor lowered himself to his seat, Lorca put her arms around him. Her breath was hot and moist on his neck.

TWENTY-FOUR

MONDAY NIGHTS WERE ALWAYS SLOW at the restaurant. Victor had already read both the *New York Post* and the *Daily News,* and now he was trapped in his kitchen cubicle with nothing to distract him from his thoughts. He stood with arms folded, reading the labels on his packages of flour and oil and icing sugar over and over again. From time to time curses came from the main part of the kitchen, where Fidel was listening to a baseball game.

In desperation, Victor set about reorganizing the utensils on his wall rack. But this could not distract him from the feeling that he had compounded his evil by provoking Lorca's sympathy under false pretences. It was one thing to simply not tell her the truth; it was another to get up in front of a crowd and actively pretend to be a victim. He had no right to any sympathy from Lorca. Victor considered fleeing: he could disappear one night and leave no forwarding address. Still a coward, he thought. Still running away.

He could not continue his deception much longer. Lorca's new look of tenderness was unbearable, almost worse than any anger could have been. Sooner or later he would have to reveal himself, and the outcome would be the same as running away: he would never see her again. He imagined the horror on her face when he told her. She would spit on him.

The owner appeared at the kitchen door. "Someone here for you, Ignacio. A woman."

Fidel, the chef, let out a whoop. "Ignacio has a girl-friend! Ignacio has a girlfriend! Bring her back here for all of us to see."

Victor ignored him.

"This woman must be blind or crazy!" Fidel shouted after him. "You give her one for me, eh?"

The dining room looked deserted. The bartender had gone home, and the owner was entering the night's paltry receipts into a ledger. A last couple lingered in a corner banquette, holding hands and staring into each other's eyes. Their waiter stood nearby, leaning back against the wall, his eyes closed.

Lorca hung back, just inside the entrance, as if fearing she would be thrown out. "I could not sleep," she said. "I hope I didn't get you into trouble by coming here."

"No, no. It's okay. It's fine."

She raised her eyebrows at the banquettes, the rich

tablecloths. "You never told me you worked in such a high-class place."

"Oh, yes," said Victor. "Very high-class." I will tell her everything tonight, he thought. As soon as there is a good moment.

It was midnight, it was Monday, and it was raining. The avenues were busy, but the cross streets were slick and deserted. A faint mist clung in webs to the street lights. Victor and Lorca walked several blocks in silence, Victor trying to work up his courage to speak. But he began to sense that Lorca too was working herself up to something, and he decided to let her speak first.

They were heading west toward Sixth Avenue, without having discussed where they were going. They crossed the avenue, and when they reached the far corner, Lorca suddenly stopped. Somewhere in the shadows a bottle smashed.

"What's wrong? Was there somewhere special you wanted to go?"

Lorca curled one hand around his neck and kissed him. Her tongue darted between his lips and out again. "I want to go home with you. Will you take me to your apartment?"

"I thought you didn't want to be kissed," Victor said, feeling a foolish grin spreading across his face.

"I was mistaken," she said earnestly. "Will you take me to your famous Royal Court?"

"We can go there, if you want."

"You don't want me to come?"

"No, no, of course I do. It is not the most pleasant place, that's all."

"I have seen worse places, I am sure."

Silence claimed them once more for the walk uptown. Victor became more nervous with each block.

"I will make some tea for us," he said when they were inside. He didn't want tea, he didn't even like tea; but it was an excuse to turn his back to her, to hide his nervousness by fiddling with the kettle and the hot plate.

Lorca stood in the middle of his single room, looking around. Victor was acutely aware of the peeling paint, the mildewed rug he had found on the street. "How much you pay for this place?"

"A hundred and fifty a week."

"Ignacio, you have no kitchen. And where is the bathroom?"

"Down the hall. Believe me, for Manhattan this is not such a bad deal."

Lorca sat down on the bed. "Anyway, I don't want to talk about rent."

"No. And I don't want any tea."

Victor switched off the hot plate and stood with hands on hips, facing her. He felt like a trapped chess piece, unable to move without causing loss.

"I don't blame you for hesitating," Lorca said. "I know I am ugly."

"Don't say that. I think you are beautiful."

She gave a short, bitter laugh.

Victor sat beside her on the bed. "You are very beautiful. It's the truth." He held her hand, stroking her forearm. He felt the ridged scar on her wrist.

"Don't look," she said. "It's ugly."

He held his hand over the old wound as if he could soothe it. He traced the jagged scar with his thumb.

"It was handcuffs. They were so proud of these handcuffs. Like children with a new toy."

He remembered the blood coursing down her body, the scarlet pool on the floor.

She stood up. "Ignacio, would you close your eyes, please? I'm going to get undressed. I don't want you to see me."

Victor turned over on his side and faced the wall. He took slow, deep breaths, trying to calm himself. She thinks she loves me, he thought. Lorca thinks she loves me, because she believes I suffered. That would be in her character. After all, it had been the suffering of another, and not her own, that had finally broken her at the little school. He pressed up against the wall so she could slip under the covers.

"Does it have to be so bright in here?" she asked. She had pulled the covers up, almost completely hiding her face.

Victor switched off the light and got undressed. Street light poured through the window, bathing the room in a cool metallic glow. Lorca turned on her side, facing the wall, when he got under the covers. He put a hand on her shoulder, feeling the small muscles tense.

After a time he exerted a gentle pressure, pulling on her shoulder. "Lie back." The command was gently expressed, but it was still a command, and it seemed to hang in the room like a garish sign.

Lorca hesitated, then lay back against the pillow, clutching the covers up to her chin.

"Let go." His voice was nearly a whisper. He stroked her forehead with one hand as he spoke. "I want to see your body, Lorca. I want to see your beautiful body."

Lorca was rigid, shaking.

"Please," he said softly. He lay a hand over the bony fingers. A pale circular mark glistened where the electrode had burned her. He touched the mark lightly with a fingertip and felt Lorca stiffen beneath him. He pressed his lips lightly to her fingers.

He tugged gently at the covers.

"Ignacio. I am so ugly."

Wordlessly, he stroked her fingers until her grip on the covers relaxed. He pulled the cover slowly away, revealing her breasts and the livid marks where the electrodes had been attached. "Oh, Lorca," he said softly. "I am so sorry." He bent forward and pressed his lips to a semicircular mark. "So sorry."

Lorca groaned like a patient coming out of anaesthetic.

Victor laid his head on her chest and stroked her belly. Her skin smelt of soap, warm fabric, and faintly of laundry detergent. Desire flowed into him, but the hard white circles on her stomach, ridged like lunar craters, checked it. He remembered her screaming, begging them to stop. He remembered the white numerals on the dial.

"I am so sorry," he said again, lightly touching a mark near the ridge of her hip bone. Her flesh shuddered under his hand.

"There's no reason for you to be sorry," she said. "You didn't do anything."

"I wish that I could take back the pain. I wish I could take it back into my hands. My lips." He began kissing each white mark, moving down her ribs. The current of desire flowed into him, stronger this time.

"No, please." Lorca took his head in both her hands and held him back. "Please, Ignacio. I cannot."

He lay still.

"I am sorry," she said. "I was wrong to come here. To expect—"

"Shh. It's okay. We don't have to."

"Everything is so ugly to me now. They did things to me, Ignacio. They *put* things in me."

She turned away from him again, and Victor stroked her shoulders and gently rubbed her upper back. His hands made wide, inexpert circles over her scapular bones. She gave a little moan of relief, and he was encouraged to continue. This was what the human body was designed for, he thought, to bring comfort to another human body. A stroke here, a caress there—it was so easy for the human hand to give pleasure, so effortless and natural. It began to seem possible that he could make up for what he had done to her. If he gave her physical pleasure every time he saw her, over a period of months, say, or even years, might he not make up for the pain he had caused her? He squeezed the narrow cords of Lorca's shoulder muscles, rubbing with his thumbs. Suddenly she gave out a loud, strangled cry.

"I'm sorry. Did I hurt you?"

The bony shoulders gave a heave beneath his hands, and there was another loud cry. Then a violent quivering, and she pressed her face into his pillow as the flood of tears, so long suppressed, broke free. Her knees drew up as if in convulsion, and she cried as hard as an infant, in huge coughs and bottomless gasps. It was an orgasm far more powerful than the kind he had anticipated, and it went on for so long that it began even to frighten him.

The tears stopped for a moment.

Victor's hand had been resting on her shoulder the whole time. He moved it slightly, giving her bicep the gentlest squeeze. "Are you all right?"

This unleashed another spasm of crying, then a respite, then a last brief aftershock, and Lorca lay exhausted on her back as if she were a castaway, thrown up onto this bed after weeks at sea.

Victor put his clothes on and made tea. There was no Kleenex, so he went down the hall and came back with a roll of toilet paper, which he handed to Lorca. The tears, he could see, had done her good. The hard set of her features had softened, and there was more colour in her cheeks than he had ever seen.

He waited until she had taken a few sips of tea before

speaking. "You must have needed to do that," he said. "Feel better?"

She nodded. When finally she spoke, it was about something totally unrelated. "The other day . . ." she began. She stopped as if she had forgotten what she was going to say.

"Yes? The other day?"

"The other day. At the church. When you spoke—when you told us what happened to you—it really affected me, Ignacio."

"I'm sorry. I should not have gone on the way I did. It was very childish of me. That woman upset me with her accusations."

"Yes, of course she did. Of course. But it hit me hard. It hit me very hard, to hear what they did to you in that place. Even for me—it was hard to believe that anyone could hurt a man as gentle and kind as you. That they could beat you, and do those things to you."

"No, no," he said hopelessly. "It wasn't so bad for me. I was just upset. I was nervous. That woman—"

"It made me so angry—I cannot tell you how angry it made me. I am going to testify, Ignacio. I am going to Washington and I am going to testify at those hearings."

"Do you think that's smart? How can you be sure it is safe?"

"Maybe it is not safe. But I cannot live like a rabbit, shaking in fear my whole life." She turned on her side and smiled at him, flashing the broken tooth. "You see? Seeing you, Ignacio—seeing how brave you are, how cheerful in spite of the pain you have suffered—this has taught me not to be afraid."

"No, Lorca. You are wrong about me."

"I am not. Now, will you turn around so I can get dressed?"

It was nearly three o'clock in the morning, but he could not persuade her to stay. She wanted to take the subway home, but he would not hear of it, and pressed a twenty-dollar bill into her hand. He waited with her in the cold, damp wind that blew up Broadway until they managed to flag a cab.

"Please think more about these hearings," he said, holding the door for her. "You are safe now. I want you to stay safe."

She smiled up at him, and then he was watching the tail lights of the taxi merge into the other lights of Broadway.

Later, he sat for a long time on the edge of his bed, clutching the pillow Lorca had soaked with her tears. She was not a woman to be talked out of anything; it was pointless to try. "It's the only way I have left to fight those people," she had said. "I am going to Washington. I am going to the hearings. And there I will tell them all about our little school."

TWENTY-FIVE

THE BIZARRE LANDSCAPE OF NEW JERSEY was behind them. Victor had never travelled on an eight-lane highway before, and he found the intricate turmoil of expressways, parkways, tunnels and bridges frightening—especially at seventy miles per hour. But the vast networks of pipes and vats, the chemical smells and the whoosh and roar of eighteen-wheelers, were over now, and the road that unfurled before them was the most beautiful Victor had ever seen.

Wyatt had borrowed a car for this trip—a cramped, rusted vehicle with a bad rattle in the engine and a powder of cigarette ash and what looked like cat litter covering every surface. Lorca sat in the back, and Victor, feeling it would be rude to leave Wyatt alone up front like a bus driver, sat in the passenger seat beside him.

"It makes sense," Victor said. "They make the roads

223

to Washington the best possible. You have to give people a sense of importance when they drive to their capital."

Wyatt glanced over at him. "I don't get you."

"We have travelled at least fifty miles, and there has not been a single hole. No patches, no dirt sections. All your highways cannot be so perfect."

Wyatt had been uncharacteristically subdued ever since they had met at the church. He just shrugged. "Most of the interstates are pretty good."

"Not like this, I am sure." The surface was so smooth, the curves and inclines engineered to such perfection, they seemed to waft the car along on a cushion of air.

"Look," Bob said, in a different tone of voice now. "What I said at the church about Graciella and the others making other travel arrangements? It's not true. The fact is, they backed out."

Lorca sat forward in the back seat. "Graciella is not going to testify?"

"No. None of the others is going to testify. There will be a few people coming from Los Angeles. Some from Minneapolis. But they'll be testifying about village raids, and about the disappeared. We don't have anyone else talking about clandestine jails. So, Lorca, your testimony is more important than ever."

"I am the only one from our group?"

"Yes. I'm sorry. I misled you."

"You lied to us," Victor said sharply.

"I'm sorry," Wyatt said—quietly, for him. "I was afraid Lorca would change her mind too."

"She has a right to change her mind. Maybe she *should* change her mind."

Lorca was still leaning forward, gripping the backs of their seats. "No, I will not change. I will testify."

"Good girl," Wyatt said, and gave the steering wheel a light slap with his palm.

Victor cursed under his breath and looked away.

Half an hour later, Wyatt pointed at the passing landscape. The hills were bigger and deeper green, with patches of yellow and blue flowers. "This is Delaware we're in now. One of the smaller states."

They travelled another thirty miles or so in silence.

Then Victor felt Lorca's hand on his shoulder, the warmth of her fingers through his shirt. He turned in the seat, and she raised her eyebrows in a quizzical expression. "What?" he asked.

But she shook her head and said, "Nothing. Nothing at all." And sat back to watch the green parade of hills, the dark clouds gathering above them.

"This is Maryland," Wyatt announced a while later. "Richest state in the union. Great for sailing—not that I've ever been sailing. Hope that rain holds off till we get off the highway."

Victor fixed his eyes on the interstate's vanishing point that shifted with each hill, each curve. "Perhaps I will write something out, Bob. Something for the hearing."

"Write what? Instead of testifying, you mean?"

"I could tell them what I did at the little school."

"If you want to testify, Ignacio, just testify. A piece of paper isn't going to do it."

"Why not? It is the same as the things I would say."

"It's not, I'm afraid. The committee allows written testimony, but it's not as effective. They can't question a piece of paper. They can't test its credibility."

"But suppose there was another witness. Another person who saw all of the things I wrote down. Who could say, 'Yes, this happened. Yes, that happened.' Who could swear that every word I wrote was true."

"They could corroborate it, you mean. That would help. That might work."

"What do you mean?" Lorca said from the back seat. "There was another prisoner with you? Someone who will give evidence before the committee?"

"There was someone there. Someone who can testify to the truth of what I write. I don't want to say any more right now."

"But there's only the two of us, Bob said. Who else do you know?"

"It's not a soldier, is it?" Wyatt asked hopefully.

"No. Not a soldier."

"Man, that's what we really need. A Guardia deserter. Someone who knows all about these jails from the other side. That would blow this thing wide open."

There was some confusion at the hotel, which was a Quality Inn high up on Connecticut Avenue. Only one room had been booked for the three of them, and it took

Wyatt twenty minutes to straighten things out. Victor and he ended up sharing a room on the third floor; Lorca got a corner room at the end of the hall.

Although the room was very plain, all of the furnishings looked new. "Have you seen the bathroom?" Victor asked Wyatt with excitement. "Take a look at it."

Wyatt dropped some socks into a drawer and went to look. "What about it?"

"It's so clean! I've never seen such a clean place."

"Hotels are like that, Ignacio."

"And they have put soap and shampoo out for us. Isn't that nice?"

"Real thoughtful. I better check in with security. Told them we'd be here by noon, and it's nearly three now." Wyatt was already dialing the phone.

Victor went down the hall and knocked on Lorca's door.

"Ignacio, look at this place!" Lorca's corner room was three times the size of the other. "Have you ever seen a bed this big? It's like something for a giant. Two giants."

"Truly. That is a big bed."

Lorca had pulled the covers back, so that the crisp white sheets resembled an acre of snow. She knelt on the white expanse and trailed her fingers over the material as if it were a tapestry.

"Bob and I have two normal beds. Very good quality, though."

"Come and try it." She patted the bed, and he sat beside her. The bedspread, he saw, had been draped over a large mirrored vanity. Noticing his glance, she said, "I hate mirrors. I don't like to see myself." She lay back, propped against four pillows.

Victor lay on his side. He was about to touch her when she pointed at the windows. "I have a balcony too. Do you have a balcony?"

"Yes. A small one."

Lorca jumped up and pulled back the balcony door; a damp gust blew in, carrying sounds of traffic and the smell of imminent rain. Victor joined her outside. The hotel faced another hotel across the street—much bigger and grander than the one they were in. "Very nice," he said. "Bob says the White House is on the other side of those hills. The White House, can you imagine?"

"The White House," she said softly. "It sounds so pretty."

"Bob says we can take a tour. They let people visit."

"The map says there is a zoo just up the street, too. I think I would rather go to the zoo."

To the east, storm clouds had massed into a dark wall. The wind tugged at Lorca's hair, flicking strands across Victor's face. He stood behind her, placing his hands on either side, gripping the guardrail. "Now you're trapped," he said, but she didn't move.

"Are you really going to write about what happened to you at the little school?"

"Yes. Tonight, I will write it all down."

"Why don't you just testify, Ignacio? That is much simpler, no?"

"Perhaps I will testify. I have to work myself up to it. Writing things down may help." The first heavy raindrops hit the balcony. By this time tomorrow, Victor thought, she will hate me. This was the way it should be; it had been stupidity to expect anything else. "I love you," he said in Spanish. "*Te amo.*"

Lorca stiffened slightly, saying nothing. She raised an arm and pointed to a black bird that hovered in the air, hanging motionless on an updraft. Victor kissed her hair, so gently she did not feel it.

She said something he did not hear.

"What was that? What did you say?"

"*Si muero,*" she repeated. If I die.

"Don't worry, sweet one. You are not going to die."

"*Si muero,*" she said again. "*Dejad el balcón abierto.*" If I die, leave the balcony open.

"You are not going to die. Not while I am here. I promise." This might even be true, he realized with a kind of wonder. He would rather die than see her harmed again. Was this where bravery had its roots, then, in love?

"It is a poem, Ignacio. A poem by the real Lorca— Federico García. '*Si muero, dejad el balcón abierto*'!"

Goosebumps had formed all up her arms.

"You are cold," Victor said. "We should go inside."

TWENTY-SIX

T HAT NIGHT, THE STORM FINALLY BROKE, flinging bucketfuls of rain at the windows. Victor sat at the tiny desk in his hotel room, struggling to put his thoughts on paper. He badly wanted to be with Lorca, but he wanted to write everything out before his natural cowardice took control of him once more.

For an hour, nearly two, he floundered. He wrote things down and crossed them out, wrote them differently, crossed them out again. How did you tell the world that you had helped to break a young boy's leg? How did you testify in the clear light of day that you had been in the car that drove that boy to his death? What was the proper way to say, *I fastened the electrodes to her breasts?* Even the least of his actions seemed an enormity when written out: *I mopped up the teeth, the blood, the hair.*

A drop of sweat splashed onto the paper, blurring the word *blood*. Victor was sweating profusely, even though the room was cool. Another drop fell, smearing the word *screams.* He slid open the balcony door a little, letting the rain hit his face. Lightning briefly lit up the street below like a flashbulb. He breathed in the cool night air; smells of concrete and rain and car exhaust filled the room. Somewhere a horn was stuck, and angry voices shouted.

He read over what he had written. *I turned the power up past three. Her screams were terrible.* He tried to write in point form, in chronological order, but his brain flashed with images, as if illuminated by the storm outside.

A knock at the door.

"Who is it?"

"It's me." Strange, how he had come to love her cracked, unattractive voice. "It's Lorca."

He opened the door a few inches.

"I was nervous," she said. "The storm. May I come in?"

"Let me come to your room in a little while. An hour or so. Just now I am writing my testimony. Trying to work up some courage."

"I won't disturb you. I will sit quietly."

Those terrible sentences—he would never be able to write them with Lorca in the room. "Give me one hour," he said. "Maybe not even so long."

The brown eyes went hard and cold. She left the doorway, and a moment later her door slammed.

With hesitations and crossings out, honesty took much longer than he had anticipated. He wanted to write simple statements of fact, but the facts were disgusting.

We starved her for three days, and then I fed her a meal full of cockroaches.

He rewrote everything in chronological order, from his induction into the special squad to his desertion at Fort Benning. Point by point, he described what had been done to Lorca, to Labredo and to the real Ignacio Perez. By the time he was finished, he had filled eight foolscap pages. He signed the last one with his real name, Victor Peña.

"Victor Peña," he muttered to himself. "Victor Peña, coward and torturer." Victor Peña. Victor Peña felt numb. Victor Peña felt like a man whose home has exploded before his eyes. Destruction beyond his comprehension.

He sat in silence for some time.

"Nothing," he said aloud, he didn't know why. And a little later, "Zero."

Through his reflection in the window, he saw that the rain had slowed. He switched off the desk lamp and his face disappeared. Now he could see clearly into the hotel across the street. On the second floor there was some sort of fancy party in progress. Black waiters in white jackets served champagne from silver buckets. No one had told Victor that Washington was such a black city; he had never seen so many black people in his life, not even in New York. Whenever you saw Americans in El Salvador, they were white.

Music drifted over from the party, Brazilian music it sounded like. He could see some of the horn players on a stage at one end of the ballroom, and several couples dancing. The scene was framed in the window like a painting, and wishing you were in it was futile. The happy scene was inaccessible to anything but longing.

The higher floors were mostly dark. Perhaps it was a slow week, perhaps everyone was at the party. In a corner room a man in shirt sleeves was talking on the phone. In another, a room-service waiter arranged a vase of flowers. Then a light went on, two rooms over, revealing a man with binoculars.

At first Victor thought the man was looking directly at him, and he shrank from the window. His own light was out—the watcher could not possibly see him—but Victor moved behind his curtain anyway. The man was wearing a cream-coloured suit and a red tie. He had a moustache, and he was talking to someone, gesticulating with his free hand. The binoculars were trained to one side, on the corner of Victor's own hotel or on something beyond it.

A peeping Tom? Such a creature would not be likely to chat with a confederate as he stared, however. Perhaps a thief, sizing up a prospective target.

The man jabbed the air for emphasis. He does that just like my uncle, Victor thought. Then the man turned slightly, lowering the binoculars.

"Mother of God," Victor said. "Oh, dear Mother of God."

The man watching his hotel was Captain Peña. Victor had no sooner recognized him than the room across the street went dark and a second man joined his uncle at

TWENTY-SEVEN

How he yearned for peace. Here he was in this great city—he could only compare it to visiting Rome at the peak of the Roman Empire—and instead of seeing the sights with his wife and children at his side, he was holed up in a hotel room with a thug.

"It looks like she's gone out," Tito said.

"She has not gone out. She is taking a shower, fixing her makeup, who knows. She has not gone out."

"So, why don't we pay her a visit right now. Give her the business. Take the rest of the night off." Tito put on a waiter's voice. "Good evening, señorita! Room service!"

Captain Peña shook his head, keeping his eyes on the corner room across the street. "We'll stick to the plan. We do it outdoors."

"Why that bitch is still alive I will never understand."

"She is still alive because the former Corporal Peña is

a world-class idiot. Not too many soldiers could miss a prisoner at point-blank range."

"He is your nephew, Captain. Otherwise, I would cross the street and kill the little scum right now. On the spot."

"Sergeant, we will stick to the plan, and you will follow my orders." This constant reining in of thugs with guns, it got to be exhausting. How he hated the war.

"Where is that coward now? His light's gone out."

"He was writing at the desk for two hours. Now he is taking a nap. Gone out somewhere. It doesn't matter. It's the woman we want."

"I still say we go over there, fix that bitch right now. Take care of it quick and dirty. Fuck this waiting."

"It's too early. There are people everywhere. We will visit Miss Viera in due time, sergeant. Take over for me now." He handed the binoculars to Tito and went into the bedroom to use the phone. He called his embassy first and by prior arrangement had them patch the call through. That way, the Hilton's phone record would show only a local call. "Hello, my sweetheart," he said. "What are you doing up at this hour?"

"Mommy said we could stay up until you called."

"She did, eh? Things have taken a liberal turn in my absence. I'll have to talk to your mother about that."

"Where are you, Daddy? Why don't you come home?" The other twin was on the other line now. He smiled at his mental image of the two of them, their dark hair shining from the bath and smelling of shampoo. They would be in their matching pyjamas: elephants and leopards.

"Daddy's working. You know I have to work long hours sometimes. I hope you've brushed your teeth."

"Oh, yes."

"And don't forget to say your prayers. Put your mother on now."

"Hello, soldier. Your little girls certainly miss you."

"I miss them too."

"All your girls miss you. How is the war treating you?"

"A little slow at the moment. I was thinking of you, wondering what you were up to without me."

"I was hemming my new dress. The girls are impossible when you're away. Such moods!"

"Like their mother."

"It's true. I wish they could be even-tempered like you. My life would be much easier. Where are you, Eduardo? I know I'm not supposed to ask."

"No, you're not. What's happened to my army wife?"

"She's fed up with being an army wife. It's when you're away that I worry the most. That's when I think the worst. Are you far away?"

"Very far. I can't tell you where." Security, discipline, these were not usually so difficult for Captain Peña, and it surprised him how badly he wanted to tell his wife where he was. He wanted to tell her he had seen the Washington Monument today, and the Lincoln Memorial. More than anything, he wanted to tell her he had seen the White House. She would be so envious. But all he said was, "I wish you were here with me, darling."

"Really? You never say that, Eduardo."

"Usually there is danger when I am travelling. This place is different. Here, there is no danger."

Tito rapped on the door. "Something happening, Captain."

"Duty calls, darling. Kiss the girls for me."

"Promise me you'll be careful. I want you back in one piece."

Captain Peña made his promises, sent his hugs, kisses and blessings down the telephone line, and joined Tito in the other room.

"She yanked the curtains suddenly. I thought you should know. It looked like something was up."

"Her light is still on. Probably she just got out of the shower. Didn't want nasty voyeurs like you looking in."

"Hah. I saw her skinny little tits when she pulled the curtain. There! You can see her shadow when she moves in front of the light. What if she doesn't go out, Captain? What if she decides to stay in?"

"We're in Washington, sergeant. She won't be able to resist going out."

"She might play it safe. Stay in her hotel room all night."

"Suppose a fire alarm were to go off? A diversion of some sort. Outdoors is best, but if we have to, we will simply cross the street and make a little social call."

"I can't wait to fix that bitch. Teach her to testify."

TWENTY-EIGHT

As he backed away from the windows, Victor's knees shook beneath him. Still a coward, he thought, no matter how I spell my name. He went down the hall to Lorca's room and banged on the door. "Lorca!" He tried to open it, but it was locked. He could hear the hiss of the shower.

A room-service waiter trundling a cart eyed him suspiciously, and Victor took the elevator to the ground floor.

Beyond the lobby, a corridor led to various business suites and conference halls. Two men in identical blue suits sat at a table, partially blocking the hall. From the suite of rooms behind them, eager voices issued. Victor told the guards he needed to see Bob Wyatt.

"You have some identification, sir?"

"No. I am a witness at tomorrow's hearing. I have to speak with Mr. Wyatt. An urgent matter. Can you find him for me?"

"I'm not paid to find people. I'm paid to keep unauthorized persons out of this area. Now, unless your name is on my list—"

A small knot of people came out of one door and crossed the hall toward another. Wyatt's booming voice filled the hall, even though he was almost hidden behind a glossy young man with very thick hair and a beautiful pinstripe suit. Victor called out over the heads of the security guards, "Bob! Bob, I must speak with you!"

Two lines of annoyance formed between Wyatt's luxurious brows. "What is it, Ignacio? I'm busy."

Victor motioned him away from the crowd, away from the security guards.

Wyatt cursed under his breath. "Ignacio, really. I don't have time for this now."

"Lorca is in danger. Men from the little school are here. They are watching us from across the street."

Bob gave a short, skeptical laugh. "In Washington? Get a grip, Ignacio. I understand you're nervous, but let's not get totally paranoid. I'll see you a little later. We're planning strategy here."

"Your strategy won't be worth anything if your best witness dies. They are *here*, Bob. They are right across the street."

"Oh, for Christ's sake. How could they possibly know Lorca is here? How could they even know she's alive?"

Victor waved his hands at the crowded hall. "Obviously because you told everyone in the world. We have to hide her, keep her somewhere safe until tomorrow."

"I can't leave now. We're wrapped up in strategy here. If you want to take it up with the reception desk, go ahead."

The pinstriped young man had been moving closer as they spoke. Now he laid a cautioning hand on Wyatt's arm. "Couldn't help but hear, Bob. If this man has legitimate security concerns, we should take them straight to Greg." He shook hands with Victor. "Roger Carey, chief coordinator."

Competence shone from the young man's features; he had the smile of a Kennedy. Victor shook his hand with relief.

"Come on, I'll take you through. It's okay, guys," he said to the guards. Then, to Victor: "Greg is our security wizard. Actually, he's the Senator's security wizard. State Department coughed him up."

The three of them passed through a living room full of flowers and fruit, as if someone were in hospital. The bedroom next to it had been converted into an office where students typed at computers and talked urgently into telephones. Carey rapped on the next door. "Greg! It's Roger!"

A voice told him to enter.

"Give me a second," Carey said, flashing his Kennedy smile, and slipped into the room.

Wyatt turned on Victor. "How did you recognize these so-called hit men? I thought you were blindfolded at the little school. How did you see them, Ignacio? How can you possibly recognize them now?"

"They took my blindfold off for the land transfer ceremony. Believe me, I can recognize them."

"From that one instance? Are you sure, Ignacio?"

"My name is not Ignacio."

The furry brows contracted. A meaty paw rose to stroke the great beard. "Oh, really. Really. That's interesting. That's extremely interesting. Maybe you'd like to tell me—"

Carey appeared at the door again and beckoned them inside.

"So what the hell *is* your name?" Wyatt hissed as they went inside.

A man was on the phone, his back to them. He swivelled from side to side in a chair with a high back, so that all they could see of him was his hair—flat, blond, schoolboyish. It was the colour of corn and flashed each time he swivelled toward the desk lamp. "Is that so?" he was saying on the phone. "Is that what he thinks?"

Victor tried to get a better look at him, but Wyatt's bulk was blocking his view. Wyatt turned to him now and said, "You're going to have to explain yourself, you know."

"Everything will be explained. Just now, Lorca is more important."

Carey watched them quizzically. The blond man was still hammering at the same point on the phone. "Well, you ask him this," he was saying. "You just ask that son of a bitch who does he think is paying the bills down there."

His words flicked a switch in Victor's memory. He could not immediately place the phrase, but it sent his nerves, already straining at the top notes of fear, up another semitone.

"No, you ask him," the man was saying into the phone. "Just you ask him: who does he think's paying the bills down there?"

The flat blond hair flashed again, and Victor remembered now. The American had said those same words to Lorca. They had echoed harshly off the tile walls of the little school: *Who do you think pays the bills around here?*

The phone was slammed down.

The man swivelled around and introduced himself to Wyatt. "Greg Wheat. What can I do for you?"

Carey answered for him. "Gentleman here thinks he saw some personnel from El Salvador. Military personnel."

"Who did?" He aimed a thin finger at Wyatt. "You? You're personally familiar with the El Salvador military?"

"Not me," Wyatt said. "Ignacio here thinks he saw them." He turned to indicate his annoying charge, but the space where he had been standing just a moment ago was empty.

TWENTY-NINE

LORCA OPENED THE DOOR TENTATIVELY, and Victor pushed his way past her. "Pack your things," he said. "We're moving."

Lorca's hair was still wet from the shower and clung to her neck in a damp tangle. She frowned at him. "Moving?"

"There's no time to talk. Just pack. Where's your suitcase?" He found the suitcase in her closet and threw it on the bed. He started heaving her clothes into it: her good shoes, a sweater, the dress she had chosen for her appearance before the committee. "Are there things you need in the bathroom?"

Lorca stood frozen in the middle of the room. Shadows he had not seen for weeks darkened her face. She opened her mouth to speak, the jagged tooth visible.

Victor grabbed her by the shoulders and shook her. "Lorca, now!"

"They have come for me," she said dully.

"Yes. They have come for you. For both of us. The Captain and one of the men. There may be others."

"I knew they would come. I knew from the beginning."

"Lorca, get your shoes on. We have to move."

She sat on a chair and reached blindly for her shoes. She started to put one on, stopped, and looked up at him. Then the question came, as he had known it must come. "How did you recognize them, Ignacio?"

"I saw them at the deed ceremony. It does not matter. The point is, they are in the hotel across the street. Right this minute. Watching this room."

"They allowed you to see their faces?"

"Mother of God, Lorca, we have to go!"

"You were blindfolded. All of us were blindfolded."

"Lorca, I was not blindfolded at the deed ceremony. Will you please tie your shoes?"

"You saw their faces, and they didn't kill you? This I don't believe."

"Fine. Stay and die."

Still she did not move. Behind the dark, frightened eyes, facts and suspicions were clicking into place. Victor could almost hear it, the sound of her world reconstituting itself.

"My name is not Perez," he said at last. "Ignacio Perez is dead. He was shot a few days before you were taken to Puerto del Diablo."

He had said it now. It could not be unsaid. He felt no sense of relief, only—once again—the sensation of stepping off a cliff. He tried to prepare himself to receive

246 | GILES BLUNT

her hatred, the way a fighter prepares to receive blows. "My name is Victor Peña. I was a soldier. A soldier at the little school."

Lorca remained staring up at him from her seat on the chair, one hand still gripping her shoe. Her face had gone pale. A terrible silence flowed from her, as if a knife had entered her ribs but the pain had not yet registered.

"These scars?" Victor showed her the knuckles of his right hand. "I got these scars when I punched you. It was me who punched you in the mouth and broke your tooth."

From Lorca, a sharp intake of breath.

"The Captain was screaming, 'Hit her, hit her, hit her.' I had to obey. They would have killed me. Everyone had to take part—otherwise, how could they trust you? I should have refused. That would have been the right thing, but I could not refuse. I was too afraid. I was not brave like you." The memory of her bravery brought tears to his eyes, but he repressed them. He had no right to tears.

"No," Lorca said. "I don't believe you. Why you are telling me these lies? It cannot be true. I won't believe."

"It's true. It was my hand on the General when they questioned you. You remember they were instructing someone? 'First you turn it no higher than two. Gradually you make it stronger.' It was me they were instructing."

She shook her head. "Why are you saying this? You are not capable of such things. All right, maybe you were in the room. Maybe they forced you to do some things . . . Where are you going, Ignacio? Come back!"

Victor went down the hall to his room. He didn't switch the light on, he didn't have to. He reached under the mattress and found the two items he was looking for, one small and light, the other dark and heavy. He crossed to the window. The lights were out across the street, he could not make out any shadows on the balcony. They would be closer now.

Lorca was sitting as he had left her, except that one hand shaded her eyes now, as if from a terrible light.

"For the first three days, I threw cold water on you. I fed you a meal full of salt. A meal full of cockroaches. One day I watched you sucking water from your shirt."

Lorca's hand moved from her eyes to cover her mouth. Her eyes went dark as pits.

"Then they raped you. *We* raped you. I lay on top of you myself."

"No," she said behind her hand. "No."

"I was the last one, that first day. The fourth one. I could not do anything because I was so sick and afraid. But I would have, Lorca. I would have. I am not like you."

"No. No, please. It's not true."

"It is true. That's how I recognize these soldiers, Lorca. I was one of them."

"It's not true. You were a prisoner."

He took hold of her hand and opened the fingers like a child's. He thrust into her palm the watch that had been ripped from her wrist. "This was my reward for hitting you that day. For breaking your tooth. Remember how they cheered? The Captain pulled this off your wrist and gave it to me."

The watch lay ticking in her hand like a bomb. Lorca stared at it dumbly for a moment, then turned it over and looked at the inscription.

Suddenly exhausted, Victor sank to the edge of the bed and hung his head. He could no longer bear to look at her. He stared at the carpet as he spoke. "Your courage changed me, Lorca. Seeing how you bore your pain. Seeing how you cared not for yourself but only for others. Ever since we hurt you, I have wanted nothing but to make it up to you. To take back the wrongs I committed. Probably I wanted your forgiveness. Not probably, definitely. I wanted your forgiveness."

"I hate you," she said softly.

"So do I, Lorca."

"I hate you more than I have ever hated anybody. I hate you more than the man who ran that stinking place. I hate you more than any of them."

"Yes. I don't blame you. But now you must run. You must run, before they come for you." He was still on the edge of the bed, his head hanging down. There was a sudden movement, and then a white light exploded in his skull.

THIRTY

Victor was sprawled on the floor near the bed. Unconsciousness drained from his skull like dishwater. His tongue would not work: try as he might, he could not make it form the syllables of Lorca's name. He pulled himself to a sitting position and promptly vomited on a lamp beside him on the floor. That would be what she had hit him with. He felt the back of his head. There was no blood, but a large lump was forming.

He crawled over to the window. There was no sign of activity in the room across the street. Placing his weight on the sill, leaning his forehead against the glass, he tried to focus on the swirl of traffic below. Beneath the first set of traffic lights, he could just see Lorca running across the road. Horns honked, and there was a squeal of brakes. The watchers would have seen her too.

The door was open a little. Leaning against the desk, the dresser, the back of a chair, Victor slowly made his way toward it. He was halfway across the room when the door swung wide, and Greg Wheat was there with Bob Wyatt and one of the security guards. The security guard had his gun drawn. He held it muzzle-up as he checked the closet, the bathroom. "Nobody else."

"Where's Lorca?" Wyatt asked. He looked frightened, and Victor was amazed that he could have ever seen anything bearlike in the fluffy beard and brows. Bob Wyatt was a stuffed animal, at best.

"I don't know where she went. She ran away."

"Well, we better find her, don't you think?"

From the moment they had entered, Wheat had been staring at Victor, looking him up and down with a contempt he did not bother to conceal. He turned now to Wyatt. "Would you be kind enough to leave us alone for a few minutes, Mr. Wyatt? I want to ask your associate a few questions."

Wyatt stood uncertainly in the doorway. "I don't know. I think maybe I should stay."

"I need you to give us some privacy, Mr. Wyatt. Just go and wait in your room, sir."

Wheat would not be armed, Victor thought. He was too high up for that.

"I'll be in our room," Wyatt said to Victor, as if he had just thought of it. "If you need me."

The security guard closed the door. By the time he turned around again, Victor had drawn his own weapon, the only thing he had taken with him from Fort Benning, and had it aimed at Greg Wheat's head. "Hand over your gun," Victor told the guard, "or I kill your boss. Don't hesitate, because I won't."

The security guard hesitated. Victor shot him, he hoped not fatally. The man lay groaning on his stomach.

Greg Wheat was backing toward the door, hands raised. "Just calm down now," he was saying. "Just take it easy."

"You're the one who told them," Victor said. "The famous reciprocal relationship. You gave them the names of the witnesses, didn't you."

"I don't know what you're talking about."

"We help you with your security leaks in Salvador, you help us with our little problems up here. It's only common sense. Or maybe you think of it as professional courtesy."

"Listen. I'm a State staffer in charge of security. I look after visitors for State. Nothing else. Don't cast me as the bad guy in some fantasy you're having, okay?"

"I recognize you from El Salvador. We didn't get many Americans at the little school. The truth is, you were the only one, Mr. Wheat."

"You're confused. I was with the State Department, stationed in El Salvador. End of story. You and I never met. I don't know anything about any school."

"Out on the balcony." Victor gestured with the revolver.

"This man needs medical attention."

"Go. Move."

Wheat backed out onto the balcony, and Victor locked the door. The man on the floor groaned. Victor picked up his weapon on the way out. He ran to the end of the hall and took the fire stairs down the three floors to the lobby.

There was a commotion around the front desk, men with walkie-talkies. The shot would have been heard. Victor pushed his way through a knot of Japanese tourists and out to the street.

He went the way he had seen Lorca go; beyond that, he had no goal other than to put distance between him and the hotel. Lorca was afraid. She was alone. She didn't know the city. Where would she go?

A block farther, and Victor came to the gates of the Washington Zoo. Lorca had said it was near. In fact, she had wanted to see it. A sign said it was closed, but the chain-link fence, though high, did not look formidable. Far down the hill, sirens wailed.

Victor found a spot half hidden by a chestnut tree where the fence had been bent inward. He climbed over, landing with a soft thud on the other side. For a few moments he crouched in the shadows. The zoo was spread out before him in a series of winding paths and one wide road through the middle. The storm had moved on, but everything still dripped with rain. Lamps glowed every hundred yards or so, but he saw no one, heard no one. Keeping to the trees, he made his way toward one of the darker paths. Somewhere in the dark, an elephant trumpeted.

He followed the inside of a stone fence. Houses and apartment buildings high on the hill overlooked the trees and paths. He wanted to call out Lorca's name, but was afraid to alert Tito and the Captain in case they had followed her.

He passed two enclosures where invisible birds squawked and chattered. They made a flapping sound like madness. Then, from farther off, Victor heard a man's laugh. Tito. How often that dirty laugh had echoed along the hall of the little school when he was about to hurt someone.

Victor moved with his pistol in hand, the security guard's weapon tucked into his belt. He kept low, behind a stone fence, taking the darker of two paths that forked away from him. A moat rippled quietly on his left. Beyond it, a dark shape moved on heavy padded feet, growling softly.

Monkeys gibbered and screamed in the trees. Victor passed a shuttered snack bar. Rough voices became audible, and Lorca's voice answering.

He rounded a stone pavilion, drew back swiftly into the darkness, and peered around the corner. Tito was laughing again. He waved Lorca's shirt over his head, as if it were an enemy flag. Lorca cowered against the rocks, trying to cover herself with her arms. A street lamp shone pitilessly down on her and turned the faces of Tito and Captain Peña into gargoyles. "Let's smash her head in, Captain. Hand me that rock. I want to knock this bitch into a coma."

"No," came Captain Peña's calm voice. "We want to prevent her testimony, not provoke a major investigation." It was strange to see the Captain in civilian clothes—a sight Victor had not seen since he was a boy.

Both the Captain and Tito were armed, though only the Captain's pistol was drawn. As Tito closed in on Lorca, Victor slipped the safety off his revolver.

Tito kicked Lorca's shin, and she fell to one knee.

Fear turned Victor's legs to water. He prayed for a lightning bolt, a bullet in the head—anything to take him out of this. Lorca was crawling away, Tito following. His shadow fell over her. The smack of flesh on flesh made a sharp report against the rocks. This time Lorca cried out. If I do nothing, Victor thought, if I run now, no one will ever know.

He started to back away. He stumbled on a rock, nearly falling. Then Lorca let out a high, piercing wail, and he froze. Sweat poured down his ribs, acrid with the chemistry of fear. A better soldier would save her, he thought. A better soldier would wade right in, guns blazing. But he had never been a good soldier.

Lorca's scream had silenced the monkeys. And the birds had gone still. There was a sound of tearing fabric. Another cry. And Tito's curses.

Victor stepped forward into the light and said, "Stop." Both men whirled round to face him, the Captain's gun glinting. "Let her go," Victor said. He thought his voice sounded not too fearful.

"Don't worry about him," the Captain said to Tito. "He was always a coward."

"Hey, Peña," Tito called. "You going to stop me? Come down here right now and try, you little faggot."

"He will do nothing," the Captain said.

"Tell the sergeant to back away from her," Victor said. "Or I will shoot."

"You're going to shoot?" It was the Captain's turn to laugh. "I don't believe you've ever fired a weapon in your life, little Victor. You couldn't stop a butterfly. You couldn't stop a flea, let alone a man. To shoot a man takes more balls than you will ever have."

Tito had Lorca by the hair now. He yanked and twisted, forcing her to the ground. Victor pulled the trigger. Fear roared in his ears, so that he did not even hear the shot. He simply pulled the trigger, and the Captain fell—knelt, rather, like a supplicant. He pressed a hand to his chest. Blood gleamed blackly on his fingers. Captain Peña's face bore the stunned, disgusted look of a man who has just lost a huge bet.

Tito let go of Lorca. He was reaching for his weapon, and Victor hesitated, his finger frozen on the trigger. He had shot two people in the past hour. It seemed impossible to shoot another. Tito was raising his gun. Victor squeezed the trigger, and closed his eyes to receive Tito's bullet.

When he opened his eyes again, a dark stain was spreading across Tito's chest. The big man clutched at the chain-link fence, lowering himself slowly, almost delicately, to the ground. He turned himself over, his head propped against the fence at a sharp angle, like a drunk's. His pistol, wavering, was coming up again. He levelled it against his other arm, sighting along the barrel. Even in his terror Victor admired such relentlessness. The sergeant was tough, you couldn't take that away from him. Tito's bullet caught him in the chest.

The trees looked very beautiful overhead, and with the animals silent now, the boughs made soothing, soughing noises in the breeze. How intricately the branches tangle, he thought. How stupid that he had never noticed before. Such wild precision in their scrawl against the clouds.

She would be gone by now. She would be safe. Halfway to the train station, perhaps. Lorca knew how to survive, she would be gone by now.

"Tell me what to do," the harsh voice said.

He knew that voice. Why could he not see her?

"Tell me what to do. You're bleeding so much, I don't know what to do."

"Come closer. I can't see you."

A shadow loomed, took shape and definition: Lorca's face, a cut on her cheek, her bare shoulders.

"Get me to the road. A taxi or a bus."

"I am afraid to leave you like this."

"It's not that bad, is it?"

"Your chest is open. Your leg is pouring blood. You took three or four bullets."

"No, no. There was only one, Lorca. Only one bullet. We will hide somewhere, and tomorrow we will testify. I want to tell them what we did to you. I wrote it all down."

"I will tell them. Show them."

"No, I want to go too. I will testify tomorrow with you."

"Sure. But why did you stop your friends?"

"Three or four bullets—is that what you said?"

"The big man. He fired at you many times. You would not stop. You would not stay down."

"I don't remember."

"You fought bravely."

"No, no. Not me."

"Yes, you. But why did you kill your friends?"

"I don't know. Maybe I was not afraid anymore. No, it wasn't that. I was afraid." He had been terrified of pain and death—he had been terrified through every minute, except for the minutes he couldn't seem to recall. You couldn't call that bravery. It must be something else, something to do with forgiveness, with loving her. No, not loving her, he knew he did not love her. Shame and sorrow and a strange, bitter longing, those had been his feelings. Not love.

"Mother of God," he said, and choked. His lungs were filling. "Even dying, it is hard to be honest." The thought made him laugh, and he inhaled fluid. Blood, he supposed.

It was not bravery and it was not love. He had pitied her and he had been sorry—but it wasn't that either. Not pity. "There were two sides," he said, and started to drown.

"Don't talk. I am going for help." Something tightened around his leg, and the woman closed his hand around the knot she had tied. A tourniquet. She got up, and the sense of her moving away was unbearable.

"Two sides," he tried to say, but it came out in a gargle. The woman—what was her name?—Lorca did not hear. Had she really gone away? Victor raised his free hand to his face and felt around. His skin was slick with blood, his hair sticky. Blood spread away from him in a black pool. Could all that blood really be his? His grip loosened on the tourniquet. The pool was spreading farther, he could see the tangle of branches reflected in his blood. The tourniquet slipped from his fingers. Let all his blood flow out. Let it all flow out and into the earth. Take it, he wanted to say. Take every drop of blood I have. There was not enough blood in the world to make up for the wrongs he had done.

Two sides, he wanted to say. There had been two sides. And, he wanted to tell her, if there were going to be two sides in this world—two sides in any matter, even if it involved bullets and pain and every chance of getting slaughtered—he had wanted, wanted all along, to be on hers.

ACKNOWLEDGEMENTS

I would like to thank my New York agent, Emma Parry, for taking up the daunting challenge of representing *Breaking Lorca*, and my editor and publisher at Random House Canada, Anne Collins, for having the courage and passion to publish a novel on such a profoundly disturbing subject.

I also owe a debt of gratitude to Margaret Atwood for her poem, "Footnote to the Amnesty Report on Torture." Her vivid imagining of a fearful man paid to clean up the torture chamber gave me my entry into the nightmare world of Victor and Lorca.

GILES BLUNT grew up in North Bay, Ontario. After spending more than twenty years in New York City, he now lives in Toronto. He is the author of four crime novels set in the fictional city of Algonquin Bay and featuring John Cardinal. The *Globe and Mail* called his latest book, *No Such Creature*, "a wonderful tale from a master storyteller."